LIPSTICK

DOM

Revised from the original novel Rainbow Heart and it's sequel Trying to Hide a Rainbow

T. STYLES

ESSENCE MAGAZINE BEST SELLING AUTHOR

Lipstick Dom

ARE YOU ON OUR EMAIL LIST?
SIGN UP ON OUR WEBSITE
www.thecartelpublications.com
OR TEXT THE WORD: CARTELBOOKS
TO 22828
FOR PRIZES, CONTESTS, ETC.

By T. Styles

4   Lipstick Dom

AND THEY CALL ME GOD
THE UNGRATEFUL BASTARDS
LIPSTICK DOM
THE END. HOW TO WRITE A BESTSELLING NOVEL IN 30 DAYS

WWW.THECARTELPUBLICATIONS.COM

By T. Styles

Lipstick Dom
By T. Styles

Library of Congress Control Number: 2015945747

ISBN 10: 0984303022

ISBN 13: 978-0984303021

Cover Design: Davida Baldwin www.oddballdsgn.com
www.thecartelpublications.com
First Edition
Printed in the United States of America

By T. Styles   7

What's Up Fam,

The moment you have all been waiting for has finally arrived! Without further interruption or delay, we present to you, "Lipstick Dom"!! (Insert Cheers and Music). I absolutely loved this story!!! T. Styles has proven once again that she can tackle any genre she puts her mind to. Get ready to fall in love!

With that being said, keeping in line with tradition, we want to give respect to a vet or trailblazer paving the way. In this novel, we would like to recognize:

BREE NEWSOME

Bree Newsome is an American activist and filmmaker who on June 27, 2015, climbed the flagpole of the South Carolinian state capitol building and took down the confederate battle flag. This brave soul had enough of what the flag stood for and how it was still on display after the Charleston church shootings on June 17, 2015, where a gunman took 9 black lives, and did something about it. Whether you are for or against the flag, no one can deny her bravery in the face of danger. We salute your Bree! God Bless you.

Aight, get to it. I'll catch you in the next novel.

Be Easy!

Charisse "C. Wash" Washington
Vice President
The Cartel Publications
www.thecartelpublications.com
www.facebook.com/publishercwash
Instagram: publishercwash

www.twitter.com/cartelbooks
www.facebook.com/cartelpublications
Follow us on Instagram: Cartelpublications
#CartelPublications
#UrbanFiction
#BreeNewsome
#PrayForCeCe
#PrayForSeven

By T. Styles

ATTENTION: TWISTED BABIES

Where you at?

Let me see you! Let me hear from you!

Join your Twisted Siblings at home via Facebook at: TWISTED BABIES' READERS GROUP.

Get to know your family and shout me out by using the name, Twisted Baby!

I want to meet you!

Love,
T. STYLES aka THE TWISTED MOTHER

#LipstickDom

NOTE TO READERS

As mentioned *'Lipstick Dom'* is based on my very first book *'Rainbow Heart'* and its never before released sequel *'Trying To Hide A Rainbow'*.

Readers who read my first novel will probably not recognize much of the first book in *'Lipstick Dom'*, just traces. Yet to me this novel feels different from my current expertise, like soft whispers of the novice writer I use to be.

But it's here...

Finished, as promised.

I can't say that I would ever do this again, rewrite a book I long since done away with.

Which is why it's here for only a limited time.

Enjoy, ladies.

Love T. Styles

PROLOGUE
PRESENT DAY

"You ain't nothing but a nasty bitch!" Drake yelled at his girl on the phone like she stole from him. "I knew you was a whore when I got with you...just thought I could change you. Even then your pussy stank more than necessary for a chick claiming she just showered."

The cell phone was smashed against Karen Jester's ear so hard that her temple throbbed as she took each insult to the heart, causing her to feel worse than she already had. Pressed in the corner of an old raggedy elevator as it rocked slowly downward, toward the deepest level of the building, she was devastated.

Just an hour earlier she'd been caught in an unsavory position and was doing her best to plead her case but he was digging in that ass with no chill. "You not even letting me talk, bay."

"Bitch, don't call me bay!"

Frustrated, her head drooped backwards and when the elevator dinged and the doors opened, she was surprised at the silence. With the exception of two cars—hers and a candy apple red Acura TLX, the garage was somewhat desolate.

"I know you don't believe me, Drake," she pleaded, as her long brown legs stretched toward her ride. Possessing the body of a dancer, even the simple act of walking was done with extreme sexuality. "I haven't given you much of a reason to trust me. Just know that it only happened once and it won't ever again."

"You fucked up, Karen. You don't get to ask for forgiveness."

She felt gut punched.

What did he want if it wasn't for her to beg?

Removing the keys from her blue Fendi purse, she deactivated the alarm to her banged out, old ass grey Ford Fiesta—that had been in so many accidents the passenger side door wouldn't open without a push and a tug. "I'm never gonna give up on you." She eased inside and tossed her purse in the passenger seat, the contents falling everywhere. "If you not in my life I don't want to live. I'm telling you the..."

"Don't say shit you don't mean," he said cutting her off. "The way I feel I'm liable to press the barrel to your scalp and do the honors myself. I ain't wit' the mental games no more."

She closed the door and exhaled. Hands resting on the steering wheel she said, "But it's true. Maybe if you hadn't fucked that other bitch this wouldn't—"

"Don't turn your shit around on me! You said you forgave, so we started a clean slate. I'm never gonna..."

His voice trailed off because her attention was suddenly kidnapped. Leaning in, she looked ahead and saw the glow from the radio illuminate the silhouettes of two women sitting in the Acura in front of her vehicle. There was tension between them— she was certain. Their bodies moved aggressively and the car rocked slightly. She couldn't make out their faces but when she placed the phone down, despite Drake talking, she could hear the faint sound of them arguing.

"You there, bitch?" He yelled from the handset.

With eyes still glued on the Acura, she placed the phone against her ear again. "Yes...but I think something's happening," she whispered.

"You just realizing that shit? Or have you forgotten that I caught you topping my brother off? In our apartment at that? You know that nigga been wanting to smash from..."

The handset drifted from her ear as she focused on the women in the red car again. When she blinked a few times she could now see that each was holding a weapon pointed at the other.

Suddenly a bright light mixed with the sound of gunfire lit up the vehicle, shattering the window. Glass flew everywhere, crashing onto the concrete. Shivering, Karen screamed and placed a hand over her mouth to muffle her cry. Slowly she picked up the phone and said, "I have to call you back." She hung up before he could respond.

Carefully she pushed her door open and slowly extended a leg out, followed by the other. She could hear her own heartbeat in her eardrums due to the deafening silence. Leaving her door ajar in case she had to double back, she crept toward the Acura to investigate.

"What am I doing?" she said to herself. "God...please help me."

PART ONE

Lipstick Dom

CHAPTER ONE
SUMMER, 1999
YOUNG DYKE

Sixteen-year-old Echo Kelly lie halfway on the corner of a mattress, naked from the waist down, she was rubbing her moist vagina on it as she gawked at the pinkness of the woman's pussy in the porno magazine before her. Having discovered how to masturbate just three months earlier she'd done it ever since, sometimes three sessions per day to the point of exhaustion. Since it was her mother's bed she had to hurry or risk Benita returning home from work and catching her ass— *literally.*

Brown toes nestled into the cream carpet, her waist moved up and down in waves, careful to apply as much pressure on her clit as possible. From the back it looked as if she was straight fucking the mattress...and loving every minute. Having done it before she was a pro, knowing exactly what moves to recreate to reap the reward...a deep orgasm.

She would've used her own bed but she shared a room with her fourteen-year-old nosey ass sister Taja who was taking a nap, after eating two bowls of ice cream, which caused the room to smell like rotten eggs as she farted in her sleep. That meant there was only one place of privacy available — the matriarch's room.

When she felt herself about to cum she maneuvered her hips in smaller circles as her body rippled with pleasure. She was so wet that the edge of her mother's bed was drenched with her cream. But the plan was to cover her dirty deeds with the comforter when she was done, while praying that Benita didn't take a sudden interest in the corner of her mattress.

When her tender vagina started to throb she lowered her head and pressed her nose against the magazine and imagined she could smell the woman's sleek pussy. Biting down on her bottom lip she moaned quietly as she felt her body heating up.

The sensation started in her pelvis before rushing toward her clitoris like a tsunami, causing her legs to vibrate in rage filled ecstasy. "Hmmmmmmmm," she moaned quietly, trying to muffle her sound. "Oh my...oh my gawd." Her breaths were heavy.

It was the best nut yet!

"You funky, nasty, bitch," she heard someone say behind her. "I can't wait to tell everybody 'bout this shit."

Horrified, she jumped up, and knocked the magazine off the bed but it was too late, Taja had seen it all. Her light skin was blushed with excitement as she eyed her older sister. This was enough blackmail material for years.

The muscles in Echo's face ticked with embarrassment and suddenly things were blurred. Still partially naked, she hustled around the room trying to pull herself together. "I was...I was..."

"Jerking off on mama's bed," Taja said walking deeper into the room. She moved toward the magazine on the floor— the page was open to the woman Echo used as her spank material. Realizing it was a woman her eyes opened wider than Echo's legs a moment ago. "Uggg...let me find out you gay! What the fuck!"

Echo yanked up her clothing and walked over to Taja. Snatching the magazine away, which happened to belong to her mother, she said, "Please don't say anything to ma. I'm begging you, T."

Taja crossed her arms over her chest. "Why shouldn't I?" she said sarcastically. "I mean what you gonna do for me because I got your ass now?"

Tears rolled down her face. "I'll do anything you want."

Taja turned around, stuck her butt out and said, "Kiss my ass."

"What?" She responded, confused at her statement.

"I said kiss my ass, you can start there."

Echo was just about to do it when Taja said, "Give me one second." After a few moments she held her stomach and released a long fart. Looking back at Echo she said, "Now I'm ready."

Humiliated, and more afraid of her mother than a big dick rapist, she lowered her head and kissed her sister's cheek. Even through her jeans she could smell the noxious sulfur odor stemming from her ass.

"Geez, Echo," Taja laughed. "I was just playing, and you did it anyway."

Taja walked toward the door, her light brown naturally long hair draped over her shoulder. Turning around once she looked into her sister's eyes, pressing as much fear into her heart as necessary. With a sly smile she walked out doing nothing to put Echo at ease.

ONE MONTH LATER

Taja may not have told their mother her secret but she told her friends....

Echo's noisy breath vibrated inside the basement in a small Washington DC apartment building. She could hear their feet scurrying outside as they chanted, *"Here, Dyke...here, dyke...where are you dyke?"* Their maniacal giggles caused her heart to pump faster as she prayed that they wouldn't find her.

When the sound grew faint a blanket of calm covered her spirit. Maybe they went about their business. After five minutes she exhaled, her warm fingers touching the cool knob. Making a decision to exit, she was startled when the door was yanked open by Harper and Aspen Symons, fraternal twins who were unaffectionately known as The Wild Ones.

Blinking a few times to adjust her vision after leaving darkness and being ripped into the light, Echo saw the leader of the small gang, her very own sister, sitting on a brick wall in front of her. She was holding Echo's blue diary, causing Echo to feel like the world was spinning.

Ever since it had become apparent that Echo was gay she made it her life's work to make her days long and hard.

Taja's light skin blushed with excitement, and the two long braids running down the back of her head looked like horns next to her evil expression.

"Why you reading my shit, Taja?" Echo yelled. "Just leave it alone!" She was fighting until Harper gripped her arm harder, applying pain the more she tried to get away.

Sweat poured down Echo's honey brown face, and her ponytail was unraveled— hanging slightly to the right. Even under the circumstances she was an attractive girl who had almost developed physically into the woman she was going to be. Plush pink lips, large eyes and curves wider than a girl her age should possess.

"She gonna give it back lesbo," Harper joked. "Just wait for it." Harper, who was so overweight her head and neck looked like one big balloon, gripped at Echo's arm harder, her nails ripping into her flesh.

On Echo's other side was Aspen, the total opposite of her twin, she was so skinny her body was void of any curves.

Unmoved by Echo's excitement, Taja opened the diary, flipped a page and began reading. Using her index finger as a marker she cleared her throat and said, '*Dear Diary, today I saw the new TLC music video. T-Boz is so fucking sexy and I wonder how she tastes. How she feels. How she smells...*'

Hearing her dark secrets revealed, caused Echo's stomach to tremble. It didn't help much that the Wild Ones were laughing so loudly they could hardly stand straight.

Taja slammed the book shut and looked down at Echo. "Geez, Echo. You still on that gay shit huh?"

"Looks like it to me," Harper laughed. "Talking about eating pussy and shit. And how a bitch smells."

Echo snatched her arm away but Harper grabbed it again.

Taja hopped off the wall when she saw the rage in Echo's eyes. "What you gonna do?" She got in her face. "Fight your little sister?"

Echo's stomach rolled like the tide, in long pulsing flips. She felt anger coursing through her body causing her muscles to buckle. Between

Taja's teasing and the blackmail she didn't know how much more she could take. She would've fucked her up a long time ago but fear held her hostage.

Suddenly she could hear their mother's voice yell, "Echo and Taja! Get the fuck in this house!"

Benita, a slender woman in her mid-thirties, sat at the kitchen table observing her oldest daughter Echo and her youngest Taja. Although the windows were open the summer heat was winning over the limited cool air causing all three women to sweat profusely.

"Somebody told me ya'll out there fighting each other...that true?" Benita forked some rice before sliding it into her mouth. Her brown hair snatched into a bun so tight, it caused her eyes to stretch up at the corners. Benita was an extremely attractive woman with fair skin and a slim build. Although she overreacted, she wanted the best for her girls.

Echo realized Benita wanted an answer and glanced at her diary on the couch. If Taja spoke of what was within the pages, or how she caught her masturbating, she feared abandonment. This feeling was so great she thought about killing Taja on several occasions just to keep her secret.

"It wasn't me, ma," Taja lied. "Echo just mad 'cause I was teasing her 'bout Nasir."

Echo was relieved she didn't say anything about the diary although it was short lived.

"Is that true, Echo?" Benita asked, nose flaring. "You getting upset about your sister teasing you over Nasir?" she paused. "Don't seem like no reason to get upset to me...Nasir's nice enough."

Taja, unable to control herself, smirked slightly but away from her mother's view.

Before answering, Echo glanced over at her diary. If she said no she was certain Taja would bring up her dirty deeds. "It's true...I guess."

Benita wiped her mouth with a napkin and said, "You know how I feel about ya'll fighting each other out on the street. Come here..."

Echo pushed the chair back and shuffled closer. Although she hovered over her mother, it didn't matter. Benita reached up and slapped her so hard Taja smiled.

"Now get the fuck up out my face." She focused back on her meal. "I'm tired of looking at you."

Echo retreated and walked toward her diary, with plans to burn the bitch or throw it away.

"Leave it alone, Echo...I'll bring it to you later," Taja smiled. "I'm gonna finish reading it after dinner."

Curious Benita asked, "What's that?"

Echo's legs buckled.

This was the moment she feared and she wondered how things would be once her mother kicked her out and she'd be homeless. If her mother didn't play one thing dykes was it and she'd made it clear more times than necessary.

"It's a book of poetry," Taja lied. "Right, Echo?"

Midnight cooled the city.

Half dazed, Echo slid toward the kitchen, opened the window and looked down at the street. Taja and Benita were sleep and she was relieved, wanting to be alone.

A blast of air hit Echo as she maneuvered her slender body so that she was sitting in the windowsill, her feet dangling outside. From her vantage point, eight floors high, she could see a potato chip bag dancing in the wind and a rat chasing another in an effort to fuck.

Taking a deep breath she inched forward again, preparing to jump.

She didn't want to live anymore and every day was a struggle. Depression gripped her because Benita was clear on her views when it came to bull daggers, dykes, butches and homosexuals— she hated all of them. Every time Benita called her name she was afraid it would be about her sexuality. Taja's constant ridiculing and teasing was weighing on her and no matter where she went she felt out of place.

She was just about to scoot to her death when in front of the building over from hers; she saw her crush disguised as her best friend sitting in the car with her boyfriend.

From where she sat she could see Mariah's long natural brown hair surrounding her vanilla colored face, and the red top she wore hung above her budding cleavage, making Echo warm in places she knew were naughty. Mariah was laughing hard and causing Echo to smile too.

Best friends since the first grade, their relationship grew stronger over the years, but not in the direction Echo secretly desired.

Not wanting Mariah to know how low she was about to go by taking her life, she quickly eased back into the window and continued to stare. Still in her thoughts she was shocked upon turning around and seeing her mother standing behind her.

"What the fuck were you doing, Echo?" she paused. "And whatever you do, you better not lie."

CHAPTER TWO
SWEET ANGER

Benita sat on the edge of the sofa looking over at Warren, her long-term boyfriend of over fifteen years. "I know shit happens," she said to him with red eyes, having cried most of the afternoon. "I know you can't always know if you'll get laid off but I can't carry on like this for much longer. I got the girls and they getting older. I need to have them somewhere safe, maybe away from D.C."

Warren took a swig of beer. "If the job market slow, what the fuck you want me to do? You know it's hard out here for a nigger. I don't have a pussy, or some dude waiting with baited breath for me to fuck up like you do."

Upon hearing his harsh words Brenda slapped him and he stood up, his 6 foot 4 inch frame shadowing hers. "What I tell you about that shit?" he asked. "Huh? You don't get to put your hands on me and not expect me to retaliate."

"Then make a man of yourself before I do!" she paused. "When we got together you promised to be a father figure, especially for Echo. Last night I caught her." She choked up a little. "I caught her in the kitchen. I think she was 'bout to jump out the window. And kill herself."

"Why would you say that?" he frowned.

"I think that Mariah girl trying to change my baby into being like her. I heard she's loose and will sleep with anything...girls included. Whatever the reason I need you here. I'll kill her myself before I let her go that way."

Echo stood in front of Mariah's apartment, glancing down at her clothing. The moment she knocked Mariah snatched the door open and pulled her inside. The daughter of a dope dealer, Mariah didn't want for anything, and their apartment made it clear. Although they had a floor model screen TV in the living room and both bedrooms, the real evidence of her people having money was the coolness of the apartment and the luxurious furniture— all leather, all expensive.

"Let's go back to my room," Mariah said, her energy seeming rushed.

"Something wrong?"

Mariah remained silent but as Echo moved deeper she knew what was wrong. Her mother and father were arguing— again.

"Rick, I don't care what you do." Janice cried from the living room. "I married you hoping you would be faithful but I realize you can't do that. All I ask is that you don't throw the shit up in my face with people from our building!"

"I fucked up...and I know you'll never believe me. But all I want to do is spend the rest of my life making it up to you." He paused. "I love you, baby...always have."

"If you love me, then why do you treat me like this?" As she waited for his response she knew it didn't matter what he said just how good he begged. She caught Rick cheating several times and those were just the occasions she knew about. Everybody on the block knew he slung dick regularly, throwing it at any bitch with a mouth or pussy.

Back in the day Rick was a star football player and women wanted him for his looks and his gift of gab. But those days long passed. At 31 he was a drunk, drug dealer and a womanizer, who had zero respect for Janice or their daughter.

"Sorry 'bout that," Mariah said as they walked into her room and closed the door. "Seems like every time you come over my folks fighting."

Echo glanced around as if she hadn't seen her space before. The color scheme was baby blue and a large king size bed fit for two adults sat in the middle of the room. Yellow chiffon curtains swayed due to the air conditioning unit blowing out a cool breeze, and the smell of expensive perfume tickled Echo's nostrils.

Echo's room may have been clean and practical but her best friend's felt like luxury. She sat on the edge of her bed and Mariah sat next to her, staring into her eyes. "I saw your sister and the Wild Ones outside a moment ago," she said softly. "Harper was asking about you and they were laughing about something." She cleared her throat. "Is it true what everybody's saying? You can tell me."

Echo stood up and walked to the corner of the room, embarrassed beyond belief. "No...they starting rumors that's all."

"Then how you know what I'm talking about?" Mariah asked, having caught her in a lie.

"Because...because...I mean..."

Mariah smiled. "I don't care if you gay or not." She paused. "Are you?"

Echo's heartbeat was thunder. "I don't know what I am. I mean, all my life I felt something was off and that I wasn't like my friends. That I wasn't like you."

"How you know how I am?" she paused. "You never asked."

Echo swallowed the lump in her throat and looked away. Was she coming on to her? Was this real? "I never been with a girl and for real I don't think I want to."

Mariah laughed. "If you ain't fuck a bitch then you definitely not gay."

Echo shrugged. "I don't like talking about this kind of stuff."

"I'm your best friend. Why not?"

"God...my mother. I know it's wrong but I can't help it either."

Mariah nodded. "I know how it feels to do stuff that is supposedly wrong. But the more I think about it the more I realize most people pointing fingers done did everything under the sun too. They just don't want us having fun." She smiled. "Whatever you are, whoever you are is alright with me. All I want to know is why all of a sudden you letting your sister and friends push you around. That's not like you, Echo."

"I've never been a fighter," she admitted. "Even before my sister caught me...caught me..."

With wide eyes Mariah asked, "Caught you what?"

Her shoulders slumped forward. "Looking at one of my mother's dirty magazines and...playing with myself."

Mariah got so excited she could hardly stay still. "See what I'm saying, your mother judging you when she got freak mags in the house. The hypocritical shit kills me!" she paused. "And you need to check Taja before you blow up one day. Trust me, I know."

"I think you're right... more than anything I'm afraid of what I might do if she keeps fucking with me. But with the shit she got over my head right now I don't know what to do."

"You should tell your mother. Then what she gonna blackmail you with?"

Suddenly the door to her room flung open and Rick was on the other side. He smiled at Mariah before giving Echo an evil look that she wouldn't soon forget. He never liked her but she didn't understand why.

As if coming to his senses, he smiled at Echo before focusing on his daughter. "I'm taking your mother to get something to eat." he stuffed his hands in his pockets and possessed the gait of a guilty man. "Listen, I know you probably heard about the chick in 2B..."

"Daddy..."

"Let me finish," he said cutting her off. "I told your mother and I'm telling you too... she don't mean nothing to me. I may have fucked her but I put food on the table here." He pointed at the floor. "And that will never change."

Mariah smiled but appeared uncomfortable. "I know, daddy..."

"I love you, Chicken Box."

"I love you too." Mariah waved and he closed the door.

"I don't like him," Echo admitted.

She smiled. "Too bad you not a fighter...then maybe you could save me." She paused and stared out into the bedroom. "Whether a woman admits it or not, every one wants to be saved." She gazed into Echo's eyes. "Let's go get Kari and Faith. I need to be around somebody whose life is more fucked up than mine."

Fifteen-year-old Kari brushed her hair carefully, her scalp tender, due to her mother pulling it roughly earlier during one of her drug induced rages. Her light skin appeared blushed, her emotions showing all over her pretty face. As tears streamed down her dirty cheeks she wondered was this all life had to offer?

She knew Wanda had an addiction and hoped showering her with love and affection would help her pull through but nothing she or her sister did worked. Wanda was an addict who enjoyed sucking the glass dick more than she did eating or loving her girls.

As she pulled her soft wavy hair off her neck she swept it into a beautiful ponytail when her younger sister Faith entered. Standing in the doorway, admiring her sister's beauty, she said, "Your hair is pretty. It always is."

Despite the favoritism Wanda sometimes showed to Kari for her being light and Faith dark, the sisters never took it out on each other. The preferential treatment didn't stop them from holding one another during Wanda's beatings or the times their stomachs growled as their bellies sunk in due to starvation. Their undying love for one another was the only reason they had to survive, and if they were going to die in each other's arms then so be it.

Kari smiled and reached out her hand. "Come...I want to do yours too." She paused. "Echo and Mariah will be here soon."

Faith moved closer and whispered, "It won't work, Kari, my hair not good like yours." Having bought into the bullshit their own community put on them about beauty she hated herself.

"I keep telling you to stop saying that shit. There's no such thing as good or bad hair...just a preference." She paused. "Now let me do it. Trust me...it'll be perfect."

Faith sat in the chair and Kari grabbed her water bottle. She sprayed Faith's shorter hair until it was slightly damp and her natural curl pattern shown through. Since neither had a perm in months, Kari's mane welcomed the attention and her hair came to life. When she was done she placed a headband on the front, smoothed her edges and stepped back. "See..." Kari said grinning. "My sister *is* beautiful." Standing behind Faith, she placed her hands on Faith's shoulders and stared at her reflection through the mirror.

The moment Faith felt her sister's touch on her tender skin she jumped. "Ouch!"

Having forgotten their mother burned her with a hot plate on her back last night, Kari was consumed with guilt. "I'm sorry, sis."

"Not your fault." Faith hugged her carefully. "Just wish I knew when it all would end that's all. When ma will stop hating us so much."

"Maybe it ain't for us to know," Kari sighed.

While Kari and Faith were in their room, their mother was on the phone in the living room doing her best to cop a fix. In and out of the house all day she soon realized that without money of her own nobody was fucking with her. As a result Wanda started showing the physical signs of not receiving her hood medication.

Encased in squalor, she pushed the clothes off the couch and plopped down. Wanda stopped caring for her home years ago. The cleanest space in the apartment was Kari and Faith's room because they worked hard to keep it that way.

Picking up the phone she dialed a number and said, "Hey, Erick...it's me again. Please say you can let me hold something until the first of the month. I ain't feeling too good."

"I'm not holding but even if I was I wouldn't give it to you."

Her eyebrows drew tightly together. "How come?"

"Cause you always begging and the moment you up can't nobody find your bitch ass."

"Erick, please...I'll even let you fuck me in the ass. Plus suck your dick all night...fall asleep with it in my mouth and everything. We friends but you know I know how you like it."

"Fuck that shit, Wanda. Everybody 'round here know that pussy condemned. You give anybody who comes within a foot of you a fresh case of herpes." He was laying into her as if they weren't a couple just six months earlier. "You used to be one of the baddest bitches in DC, now look at you."

"You ain't no better, nigger! Think you can talk down to me like you ain't on the same shit I am."

"At least I can buy my own high."

Hearing this brought her to her senses. Wanda was broke. She needed him, not the other way around. "Erick, please don't leave me like this. I said I'd do whatever."

"No thanks, Wanda, I'd rather suck my own dick."

By T. Styles   33

Wanda's body began to ache as she looked around her apartment from her position to see what was valuable enough to sell. It didn't take long to figure out she had nothing ...and then she thought a little harder.

There was something precious in her home after all.

"You might not want me but what about young pussy?"

"Fuck you talking about?"

"I got two teenage girls and they both virgins. I'll let you fuck 'em an hour a piece for fifty bucks. Now tell me you can get a better deal than that..."

"You sicker than I thought. I'ma addict but I ain't no pedophile. Don't ever call me again!" Erick hung up.

Wanda was furious he rejected her sick offer.

She kicked a dirty glass off her living room table and shoveled past the clothes on the floor to make her way into her daughter's room. They were sitting on the bed talking but hopped up when she entered. "Did my sister give ya'll money for food?"

Faith attempted to answer. "She...she—"

"Did she give you money or not?" Wanda yelled, tiring of her daughter's slow response.

"No, mama," Kari said.

"Well call her now and ask for some. I want to cook steak tonight for dinner but we broke around here." She lied.

Wanda's gritty hand grabbed Kari's as she whisked her to the telephone in the kitchen. The only reason why the lights were on and the phone bill was paid was because her sister needed to stay in touch with her nieces and couldn't rely on Wanda to take care of her own responsibilities.

Wanda lifted the handset, looked at her daughters and said, "Call."

Kari took the phone and obeyed, giving her aunt the entire lie.

The girls hated to lie to their Aunt Kim because she always came through whenever *they* needed her. A secretary for a prestigious law firm in Washington D.C., she was well off and had money to spend. Since she was not allowed inside her sister's home she had no idea how bad things were for her nieces. Had she the slightest inkling they would've been gone a long time ago.

After asking for fifty dollars and Kim promising to bring it later that night, there was a knock at the door.

"Who is it?" Wanda yelled, hoping it wasn't the landlord about the late rent.

"It's Echo...and Mariah...is Kari and Faith home?"

When Wanda opened the door, the stench of old food, dirty clothes and living in the filthy apartment for over ten years spilled into the hallway. With the door open she looked up at Echo and Mariah and shook her head in jealousy. They were far more clean and neat than her daughters and she blamed her children instead of herself.

Gazing back at her girls she said, "Kari and Faith,"— she focused back on Echo and Mariah— "Your friends here."

By T. Styles   35

The carnival was bustling with loud happy children as Taja, Harper and Aspen walked through it with not a care in the world — Harper with pink Cotton candy in one hand, and a box of popcorn in the other.

Disgusted at her greed Taja said, "You know that's why you fat as shit now right?"

Aspen busted out laughing. "She telling the truth, twin."

Harper looked at both of them and rolled her eyes. "Fuck ya'll!" she paused taking a bite of the cotton candy. "At least my boyfriend like it."

"Who? Ockey?" Taja asked with her hands on her hips.

"Yep!"

"I don't believe it. And what kind of name is Ockey anyway?"

"It's *Ohcey*...pronounced 'Oh-see, and it's a cute name too," Harper continued.

"Well how come I ain't never seen him?" Taja continued. "You making up niggas again? So you can get some boo credit with your friends?"

Harper frowned. "Aspen seen him." she looked at her sister hoping she'd back her up. "Ain't you, Aspen?"

Aspen nodded, not sounding very confident she said, "Yeah...and he's cute too."

"Well I'll believe the shit when I see him," Taja responded.

"Mark my words, one day he'll marry me, and I'll have a big ring. So big you won't be able to see my finger." She looked at her hand and imagined the day.

"Why are you so pressed to be married?" Taja asked. "Every time I turn around you talking about walking down the aisle and shit. That's why it's not gonna happen."

"Bitch, you don't know me for real," Harper snapped, wild eyes stirring around. "And don't tell me what the fuck gonna happen for me!" She stepped up to Taja as if she was about to kill.

"Aye, Aspen, you better get your sister before I fuck her up," Taja said calmly. Her breaths were heavy as she started the countdown. "One...two...three..."

Realizing once she hit five a full fight would be underway Aspen separated them. "Let's just calm down. We too close for that shit." She looked at Taja and then at Harper. "Right, twin?"

Harper rolled her eyes, "Whatever." She waved her off.

A few minutes later, after Harper's gut was thoroughly stuffed, they saw Monte Perkins walking toward them with a rack of his friends. Suddenly Harper had a new source of anger, needing it constantly. Monte and his boys were celebrating his birthday and were in a good mood until they spotted their hating asses.

"Look at this black bitch," Harper said to Taja and Aspen, referring to Monte. She tossed popcorn in her mouth.

The moment Monte passed Harper jumped in his face and looked at his four friends. "Good thing ya'll came in the day," Harper responded.

"Why you say that?" One of his male friends asked.

"Because you'd never be able to see his black ass at night," she laughed so hard she doubled over.

"Come on," Taja said snatching her away. When she looked at Monte she could tell his party was ruined. "You always doing dumb shit at the wrong time."

"Fuck him," she said waving him off. "He'll be alright."

"Let's go to the haunted house!" Taja said after seeing the sign some feet ahead. She didn't feel like talking about Monte anymore and didn't want the day ruined.

"I'm down if you are," Aspen said.

The three of them walked to the attraction gave the cashier their tickets and sat in one of the carts. Before they even moved inside Taja was already screaming, although all she saw was darkness.

And when they were finally taken into the house a skeleton dropped from the ceiling scaring all three of them. The girls laughed harder when a goon came from behind the cart and yelled 'Boo'.

Things took a turn when going further they were bombarded by flashing lights and the faces of different monsters. Although Taja and Aspen were having a good time Harper's body suddenly jerked around the cart forcefully.

After that part of the haunted house was over Taja was irritated when Harper's body continued to stiffen and jolt uncontrollably. She couldn't see her because it was somewhat dark but figured she was doing extra to prove she was scared. "Stop playing," Taja said. "It ain't funny no more."

But when they looked over at her they realized it wasn't a game...she was seizing.

"Not again," Taja said.

"Somebody help my sister!" Aspen yelled standing up. "Please!"

Mariah, Echo, Kari and Faith were sitting on the steps of their building looking out into the city. With the exception of Mariah, the foursome was outcasts who nobody liked at school. To some it seemed obvious why. Kari and Faith were dirty and broke and Echo was too quiet.

"Taja back yet?" Mariah asked Echo fanning a fly away from her face. "Because she starting shit again."

Echo shrugged. "I don't even know," she squinted due to the sun frying her forehead. "Ain't been in the house yet."

"What she do now?" Kari sighed.

"Monte was having his little party at the carnival," she continued. "Don't know the details but Harper said something smart and he left early with his crew. Saying he wanted to kill his self and shit." She dug in her pocket and removed a pack of gum. "His entire family from Virginia just came by the house to calm him down. He looked crazy...it was bad." She placed a stick in her mouth and passed the pack around.

"I fucking hate Harper...and Aspen." Faith said. "Somebody need to *kill* them bitches."

"Stop saying dumb shit," Kari said.

"It's true. I hate this fucking city too." Faith continued. "When I make enough money I'm leaving and I don't care what I got to do."

"What you running from?" Mariah asked. "'Cause in case you didn't realize there's a problem in every city. Might as well stay and deal with your shit like the rest of us."

"That's easy for you to say," Faith responded. "You live like a princess around here. Where me and my sister from, outside looks way better than anything we dealing with in the house."

"I'm so sick of you talking shit. You don't know nothing about me," Mariah said angrily. "You look at my clothes and think I'm happy." She exhaled. "What you don't know is I'd give it up in an instant to be *really* free."

"So...who going to the party at school?" Echo asked trying to break the tension. "They said *Junkyard band* gonna perform."

"Me and sis wanted to go but we don't have nothing to wear," Kari said. "No way am I rocking that same black dress I wear to everything."

"Got holes in it anyway, from when mama cut it remember?"

Kari nodded.

"Don't worry 'bout clothes," Mariah said waving her hand. "I'll make sure daddy buys enough stuff for all of us."

"Oh my God, that's so nice," Kari said. "You always look out."

"Don't know why it's so nice," Faith said. "All of our money go to her father anyway since mama on that shit. Technically her dough is ours."

"Wait...so it's my fault your mother a crack head?" Mariah questioned.

"Bitch, who you talking about?" Faith snapped.

"Your fucking mother!" Mariah snapped back.

"Let's just drop it," Echo said loudly. "We got enough niggas hating us as is. Ain't no need in fighting each other too." She paused. "Besides, everybody out here know your mama on that shit so don't get mad now."

"Still don't like to hear it," Faith said rolling her eyes.

When a black Chevy Pickup pulled up to the curb Mariah rushed down the steps and toward it, while the three of them watched. The driver was a handsome New York transplant named Lonzo. He was also Mariah's boyfriend.

With the sun beaming on his truck, making it sparkle, Echo found it tough to bite her tongue. "I hate that mothafucka. He always rolling up on the block like he from 'round here."

Kari and Faith giggled.

"Do you know that's the only time you show emotion?" Faith said. "When Lonzo rolls up on the block."

"Leave her alone," Kari said.

"It's true...if that's all it takes we need to see more of that nigga because you been acting soft as shit lately. Like you scared of something."

"You don't know what you talking 'bout, Faith," Echo said. "So let it go."

"I'm serious...you know you like her," Faith continued. "Might as well tell her how you feel and get the shit over with."

Since that was the first time Echo's friends talked to her about her sexuality she was shocked. Did Taja get to them too? "Where you hear that from? That I like girls? 'Cause it ain't true."

"Does it matter?" Faith continued.

Having heard her truth out loud made her ill. "I don't know where you heard that shit but stop the lies here. Mariah is a friend just like you both are."

"Yeah right," Faith giggled.

"It's true. The only reason I don't like Lonzo is 'cause he don't treat her right. How many times have we caught her crying because the nigga won't answer the phone when she calls? Real niggas don't do stuff like that. And that's why I don't fuck with him."

"Say what you want to keep you asleep at night. But I do know this, you can't compete with money," Faith continued. "And a nigga like Lonzo gots lots of it. Now you could always kill his ass. Or get with Nasir's obsessed ass and trick on him to give you some cash. Because Mariah not gonna be with no broke nigga or bitch."

"Leave her alone and stop talking like that!" Kari yelled louder. "You get so messy when you get outside. Besides, you and me both know you not living like that."

"Stop babying her," Faith continued. "You part of the reason why the Wild Ones keep coming at her neck." She looked at Echo. "You know I fucks with you. But at some point you gotta give up the meek shit. Nobody in DC respects it."

"Speak of the devils," Kari said as she glanced at the horizon and saw Taja, Harper and Aspen bopping toward them. Harper, being used to seizing, bounced back from the incident at the carnival just in time to cause more problems.

"I can't believe that bitch is your sister," Faith said cracking her knuckles.

"Me either..." Echo responded softly.

When the Wild Ones and Taja stepped to Echo, Faith, always ready for a fight, jumped in front of her. Kari did the same.

"What can I help you bitches with today?" Faith asked, ready to misplace her disdain for life out on their faces.

Taja stood planted in place and laughed as the Wild Ones circled them as if they were prey. "Come on, Faith...what you gonna do to me accept get your ass beat?"

"Name one time you beat my ass, Taja and I swear to God I'll let you do it again." She slapped her hands together. "I'll wait..." She whistled.

The Wild Ones laughed and stood behind Taja.

"You ain't gotta let me do nothing, funk box. When I get ready to drop you, you'll know it." The three of them moved in a bit closer.

"Take one more step and I'll tear ya'll to pieces," Faith winked. "Make my day, redbone."

Always the peacemaker Kari said, "Why don't ya'll just go somewhere else...damn. We chilling over here and minding our business."

Taja looked at Echo who looked down at the ground. "Let me guess...you two bitches is protecting my big sis because she told you she was gay." She laughed. "Damn, Echo. You got three bitches now? Even though you a punk you must be doing something right."

"I'm starting to wonder about you, Taja," Kari said. "You so concerned about what Echo doing, makes me think you roll that way yourself."

"You right sis," Faith laughed. "So, Taja...is it true? You down with a little incest?"

With that statement Taja brought a clenched fist on the bridge of Faith's nose promoting a full-blown fight. Seeing the situation escalate, Mariah left Lonzo sitting on the curb while she rushed to help her friends do their thing. "Here we go again," Mariah yelled.

CHAPTER THREE
FIRST LICK

Echo watched Mariah wipe blood off her face, in front of her long mirror with a tissue as Echo sat on the edge of her bed. She was hungry and her stomach rumbled but she wanted to spend every minute with her best friend before going home to eat. "I'm sorry," Echo said under her breath. "That I didn't help."

Mariah tossed the soiled tissue in the trash, smiled and walked over to her. Taking a seat next to her she placed her hand on Echo's thigh. "There ain't nothing to be sorry about." She shrugged. "Besides, you too pretty to fight."

Echo felt dumb and knew Mariah was trying to make her feel better about her punkish ways. She would've helped her friends but shit was bad for her at the time. The blackmail package Taja hung over her head arrested her moves, making it difficult for her to do much of anything. "You know that's not the real reason, Mariah." Echo admitted.

"Then how long are you gonna avoid putting her in her place? Because she act like she's having the time of her life."

"You right, but what I don't know is why." She exhaled. "When our father left it seemed like it got worse. Like she blames me or something." She paused. "I thought about what you said too, about telling my mother. But if she hates me I don't think I can handle it."

Mariah nodded. "If she does then that's her hang up, not yours. I myself can't get enough of you."

Upon hearing her words Echo felt sweaty and could hardly catch her breath. It was one thing to have a crush, but to have your crush acknowledge you unexpectedly was overwhelming. "I...I don't know what to say..."

"Say nothing...it's not necessary." She looked deeply into Echo's eyes with seduction. Slowly Mariah leaned in and kissed her, slipping a little tongue in between Echo's plush lips. Not knowing what to do with her hands, Echo touched Mariah's shoulders before allowing them to drop at her sides. She never been with a girl but it didn't seem to stop Mariah from going hard.

Slowly Mariah pulled back and said, "You taste good, Echo. I always knew your lips would be soft...but this..." she kissed her again.

Echo's body trembled and her teeth rattled softly.

Sensing her fear Mariah looked at Echo's lap and back into her eyes. "Since your lips are sweet, I wonder what else tastes good on you." She stood up, dropped to her knees and wiggled between Echo's legs. She could smell the scent of the day fuming from her body and loved every minute of it.

"Please don't...I..."

"Don't be scared, Echo. I see how you look at me." She raised Echo's shirt, pushed her bra cup to the side and kissed her right nipple. "Let me please you. I know you want me...and I want you." She ran her warm tongue over Echo's breast causing it to perk up. "You'll be my little secret."

"I never did this before." Echo was hyperventilating. She was also fidgety and felt as if she were about to vomit. Every portion of her body seemed to awaken and she wasn't prepared.

"You told me...and I haven't done it either," Mariah said through heavy breaths. "But I want my first time to be with you."

She ran her warm tongue around Echo's nipple and tiny shivers of energy coursed between her thighs, up her back and over her scalp. It seemed like every part of her body was sensitive to touch, and Mariah was just getting started.

Slowly Echo's head dropped backwards as she continued to enjoy how good her friend was making her feel. It was her first experience and if the universe was willing she hoped it wouldn't be the last.

When the soft suckles ceased, Echo slowly opened her eyes and looked down at Mariah, wondering if she'd done something wrong.

Was she too sweaty?

Whatever the reason for the pause Echo was willing to rectify it immediately, even if it meant going to the bathroom and cleaning up. Besides she could feel herself about to cum. "Something wrong, Mariah?"

When Echo followed her stare she saw Rick, her father, standing in the doorway. Caught dyke-handed, Echo jumped up and pulled her shirt down trying to think of a lie to explain the gay away but nothing came to mind.

Mariah rose off her knees and backed up also, toward the window, next to Echo.

He shook his head in disgust. "So you a dyke," he said angrily to Echo. "And now you've changed my baby girl into a dyke too!" he paused. "I knew I didn't like you."

"Daddy, it's not..."

"Shut the fuck up!" he yelled pointing a long finger in her face.

Mariah jumped, and bumped into Echo.

"Don't say anything else to me!" he walked over to a chair and sat down. "Is this what you like?" he pointed at Echo. "Pussy?" He waited for Mariah's response.

"No daddy...we were just fooling around." Her lips quivered.

His brows lowered. "How come I don't believe you? Because you looked like you were enjoying yourself to me."

Silence.

"Well...if you got a little gay in you, you know how I have to get it out right?" He unzipped his pants and stroked his already stiff penis inside of his boxer shorts. Truthfully what he just saw turned him on. "Get over here, on your knees."

Echo was horrified. What the fuck was happening?

Mariah's eyes widened as the object of her problems revealed itself in front of her best friend. "Daddy, please...not in front of..."

"Get the fuck over here and don't make me say it again!" He pointed at the floor.

Mariah trembled as her eyes flooded with tears. Turning around she looked at Echo and said, "Go home." She wiped her wet face and appeared to be tough. Shaking her head she said, "I'll be fine..."

Anger, something Echo normally didn't feel suddenly coursed through her veins. Her darker side was being awakened and it was so strong it scared her. Within seconds she envisioned slicing his throat or tearing out his eyes yet she couldn't move. "But...he...making you..."

"Echo, please leave," Mariah pleaded. "I'll be fine." She nodded although her facial expression was riveting in emotional pain and embarrassment.

Echo glared at him.

"Don't make her say leave again," Rick said.

At a snail's pace, Echo moved toward the door and before leaving Rick said, "I don't have to tell you to keep this a secret do I, Echo?" When she turned around Mariah was already between his legs sucking his dick. "You don't want me telling that religious mother of yours that her oldest daughter is butch. Because I can only imagine what she'll do to you. Which would be nothing compared to what you would have to deal with from me. Or what I would do to Mariah." He closed his eyes. "Now get the fuck out of my house."

Rick had Echo fucked up!

She stormed into the house just before the streetlights came on, but to her surprise her mother wasn't home. Taja, whose lip was busted in the earlier brawl, stepped up to her ready to start shit.

"I can't wait until, ma get's home. I'm gonna tell her how—"

Her sentence was cut off when Echo pushed her so hard that her lower back slammed into the kitchen table. It was the first time Echo ever acted out violently since she blackmailed her.

"Stay the fuck out my way, Taja," she warned. "I'm not in the mood and I don't want to kill you. But if you keep fucking with me I can't call it."

Later that night Echo sat up in bed knowing she would have to deal with one form of drama. Whether it be Taja telling her mother how she pushed her, or Rick alerting Benita that she was gay, she felt an overwhelming sense of dread.

She was about to stand up and face her problems when Taja walked inside the bedroom. "Ma, says it's time to eat. Plus we got company." She eyed her oldest sister closely feeling she'd changed overnight. .

Echo looked at her bruised face. "You told her about the fight?"

"No," she said softly. "And if she ask you gotta tell her I fell rushing up the steps to get inside before the street lights turned on."

Echo felt relieved but she knew she wasn't out of the woods just yet.

"What happened today?" Taja asked, for the first time sounding genuinely concerned. "Why you look like...like someone hurt your best friend when you came in the house?"

She took a deep breath. "Because they did," she said getting up and walking into the living room.

Once there she saw Nasir and his mother Angela sitting on the sofa. Echo's stomach grumbled because her mother had been trying to get them together for the longest. At first Echo didn't know why she wasn't interested in him. Everything about Nasir was right—he was handsome, stylish and came from drug money. But he wasn't a girl and until the past few days she thought it was something else.

It was also whispered that Nasir and Angela were bipolar, flopping in and out of moods like the second hand on a clock. Nasir's father Keith Case wasn't any better. As a hit man for medium sized drug dealers he was hardly home, leaving his son in the care of a woman who was far from stable.

When Nasir saw Echo he stood up and walked toward her. His expression resembled a boy who stood before his crush begging her to like him, and Echo felt sorry for him. "I was wondering where you were..."

Echo remained silent.

"Open your mouth, Echo," Benita said softly. "Nasir is trying to be nice."

Echo looked at her mother, Taja, Angela and then Nasir. "I ain't hungry. I'ma leave ya'll to it though." Although she was starving earlier, her appetite had been stolen after seeing Mariah with her own father. She exhaled and walked back into her room, having zero fucks to give for any of them.

If her mother liked Nasir so much she could fuck him herself.

The next morning Echo was standing in front of her mirror, getting ready for school, when Benita walked into the room with an attitude. Taja was already outside, which left them the alone time that Echo didn't desire.

"Echo," Benita said softly, closing the door. She stepped up to her and looked into her eyes as if she were trying to get the answer for her question before asking. "What happened last night? I've never seen you that disrespectful."

Echo walked away and sat on the edge of the bed to put on her shoes. "Just didn't feel like eating. Or talking."

"But why treat Nasir like that?" she paused. "He's a good kid who—

"I'm not interested in him, ma." She looked up at Benita.

"But why?"

She sighed. "Ma, can I ask you something?"

"What is it?" she turned around and sat on the edge of the dresser.

"Why you keep bringing him here and forcing me to talk to him? When you know I don't like him."

Benita looked guilty. "Because Taja has a boyfriend and I figured..."

"But I don't want a boyfriend," she said softly. "Plus you know Nasir goes to my school. If I want to kick it with him I know how to reach him, I'm not a kid no more, ma. Maybe you should stay out of it a little."

Having witnessed her combativeness up close Benita frowned and walked closer. "Then what do you want if it ain't a boy?" she paused. "Because Nasir is a handsome and it don't get much better than him. Not for you anyway." She paused. "Now I know you spend a lot of time with them little girls around here, but you shouldn't. God wants man to be with woman and you'd do well to remember that."

"Wow...it's good to know you think so little of me." She shook her head. "That Nasir is the best I can ever get."

"That's not what I mean. You're beautiful but you could do a little more to make yourself presentable." Now she was really going on her. "Maybe then you wouldn't be..."

"Be what, ma?"

Silence.

"Ma...what do you mean? Be like you? Fighting with a man I don't want every night?" she paused. "If that's all I got to look forward to I'm not interested."

Benita walked up and slapped her so hard her face burned. "Don't talk back to me! Now I'm trying to do the best for you and your sister and I don't expect you to understand. Maybe when you get kids of your own that'll change. But for now I'm the law in this house and I demand that you abide by my rules." She walked toward the door. "Now hurry up and get dressed. Your sister's downstairs waiting."

Warren was sitting on the edge of the bed looking at Benita when she stormed inside their room. Having heard the conversation, he was frowning and looking at her with extreme disapproval. "You wrong for what you doing."

She rolled her eyes and walked to her closet to grab her waitress uniform. Tossing it on the bed she said, "You don't know nothing 'bout girls. So let me handle them."

His temples throbbed. "First you want me to be their father and now you don't." he paused. "You don't want no man around here, Benita. What you want is someone you can tell what to do when it suits you. And someone to blame when shit don't go right."

"Drop it, Warren!" The vein on her forehead pulsed.

"You and I both know Echo's gay, Benita. And if you keep pushing her away you'll lose the bond. Is that what you want?"

She whipped her head toward him. "So you think it's right for girls to be with girls?"

"That ain't what I said. I was clear on my stance. Stop doing everything in your power to push your own child away." He paused. "If you ask me I think you're more embarrassed about what people may think than anything else. Especially your friend Katie you be gossiping with all the time."

Benita stomped toward him, her face flushed red. "I want you out of my house by tonight." She walked toward the door. "Be here a minute longer and you don't want to know what I might do." She walked out.

Echo walked outside and saw Harper and Aspen talking to Taja alongside the fence. Harper had a box of *Goobers* candy in her hand and an empty box of *Mike and Ike's* that she just finished eating rested on the ground at her feet.

The moment the Wild Ones saw her they thought they would have some fun at her expense but Taja deaded it quickly. "Let's go 'head to school."

"Why?" Harper joked. "Because she looking all mad and stuff? When we start giving a fuck?"

Echo looked deeply into Harper's eyes. She was already in turmoil about her mother forcing her to be something she wasn't and what Mariah went through the night before. Quite simply she wasn't up for none of Harper's fat ass foolishness.

Harper started to fuck with Echo anyway but something told her that now was the wrong time, so the three of them walked on.

With them out the way, Echo hit it toward Kari and Faith's apartment. The moment she bent the corner she saw Kari walking outside, rubbing her arms, with her book bag hanging open. Faith was behind her and a bloody Band-Aid was stuck to her face.

Echo immediately knew they were abused again.

But instead of asking questions she walked between them, placed an arm around Faith's shoulder and the other around Kari's as they continued silently to school.

Life in the hood was draining.

Since Washington D.C. didn't have school buses, especially for high schoolers, Echo, Mariah, Kari

Lipstick Dom

and Faith walked down the street on their way home. Earlier in the day Echo was uncomfortable around Mariah, because of the rape she witnessed by the hands of her own father. But a few hours later, she did her best to push it out of her mind, as Mariah appeared to have done.

"So, Mariah, you still singing at the party this year?" Echo asked. "Because that's the only reason I go."

"Maybe," she said. "It depends on if my father—"

"Fuck that nigga," Echo blurted out. "He ain't no real father. He ain't nothing but a creep."

Mariah's eyes widened and she looked back at Kari and Faith who wondered what caused the spark of anger on Echo's part. Quickly Mariah pulled her to the side and whispered, "Echo, please don't do this in front of them."

Anger coursed through Echo's veins. "Do what? Tell them that your father made his own daughter suck his dick? And that I had to watch it and can't do nothing about it?"

"It's my problem. Let me handle it."

"Handle what?" Faith asked, the blood stained Band-Aid on her face hanging off slightly. "What ya'll talking about on the down low now?"

Mariah focused back on Echo, who she could tell was about to let them in on an intimate secret. "Please, Echo...I'm begging you. This shit ain't for them."

"It's nothing," Echo lied to Faith. "I'm just not a fan of her pops that's all."

Faith stopped walking, causing the others to stop too. "So that's what we do now?" she paused. "Lie to each other?"

"It ain't about that," Mariah said. "Ain't about you either. So drop it."

"Yeah, Faith, let it go," Kari said. "It ain't like we don't have enough problems of our own." She paused. "So what's up later? We still spending the night at your house, Mariah?"

"No!" Echo yelled. "I mean...we shouldn't be spending nights over Mariah's crib all the time." She looked at Mariah. "Her parents probably want their privacy. Ya'll can stay at my house though."

"Fuck that!" Faith snapped. She was still salty about the secrecy between Mariah and Echo. "I'm tired of this bourgeois ass bitch looking down at us from her pedestal. I mean how come Mariah's allowed to know our business but when it comes to hers she's so private?"

"What the fuck are you talking about now?" Mariah snapped.

"You ain't got no problem saving me and my poor little sister from our drug addicted mother, but the moment we want to know your darkest secrets, shit's off limits. Be real...you think you better than us don't you?"

"Ease up," Echo said. "It's deeper than you realize."

"Then why don't you tell us about it?" Faith asked. "If we supposed to be friends."

"Because it ain't my story to tell, Faith, even if it was and I don't want to," Echo responded.

A white baby Benz pulled up with the top dropped and parked alongside of them. Inside of the car were Claire and Victoria. Mariah's fly friends. They came from money too and with Mariah the three of them were the most sought after teenagers in their high school.

The moment Echo, Faith and Kari saw them they rolled their eyes.

"Mariah, you do charity on the weekend, must you do so after school too?" Claire asked referring to Mariah hanging around Echo and the crew. She ran her fingers through her natural shoulder length black hair before resting her hand on the steering wheel.

Faith and Kari threw the fuck you finger in the air.

Claire and Victoria laughed.

Mariah stepped closer to the car. "We were just going by Echo's house for a little and—"

"Save the shit," Victoria said, as she played with one of her long thick brown braids. "Get in the car. The fellas waiting on us at the clubhouse. They got drink and smoke and I'm not even gonna lie, I need a buzz. Get up with the misfits later."

Mariah turned around, looked at Echo and the crew and eased in the back of the car. In lieu of saying goodbye she waved until she was out of sight.

Echo, Faith and Kari continued to walk. "I don't know why we keep letting that bitch roll with us," Faith said as she kicked a rock. "As long as we are who we are, she will always pick them over us."

"You know what your problem is," Echo yelled. "You're jealous! You also think you the only one who goes through shit! Don't let her fly clothes and pretty room fool you! She got it as bad as we do...if not worse. I'll get up with ya'll later." She stormed off.

CHAPTER FOUR
PINK WET LIPS

The Saturday sky was bright blue and offered a cool breeze as Echo, Faith and Kari sat on Echo's porch, sharing a big bag of Sour Cream & Onion potato chips.

After eating her fill Faith stood up, brushed the crumbs off her grungy clothing and leaned up against the fence causing it to squeak. Sticking her little fingernail into her tooth she asked, "Anybody seen Mariah since earlier this week?"

Kari shook her head no. And although the answer was the same for Echo, she could provide them with the minutes and seconds because for her it felt like an eternity. They never went so long without talking.

"I called the house the day she got in the car with Claire and Victoria but the phone kept ringing. Thought something was wrong at first until I saw her at school on Monday." She looked at the ground. "She didn't even speak."

"I don't know about ya'll but I'm cutting fake bitches off this year," Faith admitted. "That's my only mission...starting with her ass."

Kari sighed. "It's amazing how you love talking about her, when outside of Echo she's the only one who looks out for us."

"And for that we should kiss her ass?"

"No! It ain't about kissing ass! It's about being loyal, Faith." She looked out into DC. "When you have real friends in your life the last thing you should do is your best to get rid of them." She shook her head. "It ain't like nobody else beating down our door to chill."

Just as she said that a cute little red Honda Accord with paper tags parked in front of the building. The three of them kept their gaze on the car, wondering who would slide out. Within seconds Mariah eased out with a bunch of shopping bags in her hands. With a huge smile on her face she raised them in the air and said, "It's Christmas time in the city!"

Kari was excited about the contents of the bags but Echo was just happy to see her— and that she was talking to them again. She took inventory of her own tight jeans and her black sandals and fresh polished nails to be sure she looked presentable.

Mariah looked like she was floating as she made her way down to them. The moment she was within a stone's throw of the girls Faith laid into her as usual. "Where the fuck you been fakey?" Faith asked.

Mariah's smile vanished. "Why you gotta keep coming at me like that? Huh? Why can't some days be chill?"

"Because fake bitches need to be dealt with accordingly." She rolled her eyes. "Like I said...where you been?"

"Well tell me if I'm still fake now." Mariah dug into the bag and pulled out a beautiful black dress and some cute sandals. "This is for you, for the party."

Faith looked at the cute outfit, rolled her eyes and stormed away.

"What's wrong with her this time?" Mariah asked stuffing the dress back into the bag.

"It doesn't matter," Kari said, grinning. Her eyes were glued onto the bag. "Got something in there for me?"

Cheesing again Mariah said, "For you my friend I have this..." she reached in the bag and pulled out a red dress with a pretty pair of matching heels. "You gonna look so hot in this shit. I started not to give it to you because I wanted to sport it."

Kari placed the DKNY dress against her frame and was so excited she could hardly stand still. She never had a designer outfit and her body trembled just thinking about how she would look wearing it. Wrapping her arms around Mariah's neck, Echo caught the whiff of her underarms. Although Echo and Mariah looked at one another after breathing in the smell it wasn't out of malice, it was out of sadness because they loved her so much and wished Wanda did a better job by her children. Each knowing it would never happen.

"Thank you so much!" Kari said excitedly. "How can I repay you?"

"Bitch, please...we sisters," she winked. "All I want is for you to have a nice time at the party." She paused. "The three of us are going together, I'm renting a limo. Faith too if she can get some act right.

"What about your friends?" Echo asked. "I heard you were rolling with them."

"You ain't heard? I cut them bitches off," she winked. "They gave me an ultimatum so I chose correctly."

Seductively she stared into Echo's eyes. Normally Echo would turn away but this time she maintained her gaze until Mariah blushed and looked away.

Echo was gaining her confidence and control and it felt good.

"You don't know what this means to me," Kari said. "I never had nothing like this."

"It's cool, Kari...really. We family."

Mariah focused on Echo. "I have a dress for you too but I got to give you something else first." Quickly she took her by the hand and led her into the building. When they were in the corner of the basement downstairs, she pushed Echo up against the cool dirty wall and pressed her tongue into her mouth.

Done with the game of being shy, Echo snaked her hands under Mariah's shirt, the feel of her soft breasts in her palms made her pussy moisten. Although she masturbated often it wasn't the same. Mariah knew how to handle her and she loved every minute of it.

Just when Echo thought it couldn't get any better, Mariah wiggled her fingers into her jeans, around her panties and into her warmth. When she felt the slickness of Echo's pussy Mariah exhaled deeply. "Oh, Echo...you feel so good." With heavy breaths she asked, "Why are you so fucking wet?"

Slowly she removed her hand and licked Echo's juices off her fingertips, driving Echo insane.

"Aye, ya'll, the Wild Ones are coming down the block!" Kari yelled into the hallway. It was as if she knew the dirty things they were doing in the basement and wanted to keep them from getting caught. The cool shit was nobody told her to be on lookout but she did it anyway. Real friends didn't need instructions.

Heeding her words they pulled themselves together and rushed back outside. The moment they exited the building the Wild Ones were standing there, out of breath and looking crazy.

"Ya'll gotta come quick...some girls just jumped Taja," Harper said. "And it don't look good.

All the car windows were down in Mariah's new ride because Kari, who was sitting in the backseat with Taja, arms stank so badly it was difficult to breathe without a little air.

Mariah was in the driver seat and Echo was in the front trying to make sense of what happened.

"I'm not understanding...why would some northeast bitches jump you?" Echo asked looking back at her sister, secretly knowing that this would happen sooner or later because of her attitude and mouth.

"Furthermore why would your friends bounce?" Mariah asked. She adjusted the rearview mirror so she could see her bruised face. "As much shit as them bitches talk they never should've left your side."

Taja rolled her eyes and leaned back into the seat. "One of the girls who jumped me fucking my boyfriend or some shit like that. Had I known he dealt with the ugly bitch I would've cut him off but he lied."

Everybody shook their heads. "So what you gonna do now?" Echo asked. "Fight them back?"

"Why?" Taja snapped, embarrassed more than anything. "It ain't like you gonna do nothing but run anyway."

"Why the fuck you mad at Echo?" Kari snapped. "If it wasn't for her, me and Mariah would've never run up on them bitches while they were still kicking your ass."

"Wasn't nobody beating my ass."

"You keep believing that shit if you want to," Mariah said.

"What I want to know is why your girls leave?" Kari asked. "They ain't got no problem fucking with Echo but when it come to fighting somebody else they fall short."

"You know what..." Taja opened the car door. "I don't know why ya'll faking like ya'll give a fuck 'bout me anyway." She eased out. "I'm going in the house. Consider your charity work for the day done." She limped off, holding her stomach.

When she was gone Kari said, "You think they jumped her for another reason?"

Echo shrugged. "Who knows with my sister."

"I know this, I'm gonna give the Wild Ones the blues at school tomorrow," Kari said. "Make sure everybody know they punks in real life, especially Harper."

"Please don't...the last thing we need is them taking it out on you...or Faith," Mariah said.

"Like we give a fuck." Kari sighed and grabbed the new dresses Mariah bought for her and her sister. "I'm gonna leave ya'll to it though." She opened the door. "Thanks again, Mariah. You literally made my day."

"Before you bounce...don't tell anybody that me and Echo were in the basement earlier," Mariah suggested. "You know how rumors start."

"I don't know what you talking about," she winked before leaving.

When she left Echo said, "I guess she knows..."

"What's to know?" Mariah asked checking her hair in the mirror.

"About us...that's why she left just now. Why else would she leave? You know she doesn't like being in the house longer than she has too."

Mariah turned toward Echo and grabbed one of her hands. "You didn't ask about my new car." she paused. "How come?"

Echo realized she hadn't. "I guess I forgot...who bought it for you?"

"Lonzo," she said softly. "He got tired of me walking and wanted me to have wheels. That's what real niggas do...they provide for their women. You understand what I'm saying?"

Echo felt her body trembling. "If I could buy you a car I would. But I'm in high school and I don't sling rocks...what you want me to do? Get a job? Because I will...just say the word."

"It ain't about that, Echo. It's about being with a nigga who can look out. It's about being taken care of properly. With the money Lonzo got we can do us on the side and he would never know."

"So...so what are we doing?" she stuttered. "What was all that in the basement?"

"It was us playing around, E. You know I can't tell nobody what we do. Besides I'm not gay. I just like being with you." She touched the side of Echo's face. "You'll be my little secret...*remember?*"

Echo laughed. "Your little secret? Why the fuck you keep saying that shit?" she popped. "I love you, Mariah. And I always knew it but after seeing how you look at me I know you feel the same. I'm not a dude and I'll never be. But if you be with me I will work hard so that you don't have to trick on no nigga for a car. Or your father for a couple of dresses. You mean more to me than that."

Mariah looked down into her lap and back into her eyes. "Now I see what your sister was saying. You coming at me hard on this dyke shit." She looked away. "Echo...Maybe we should slide back from each other for a little while. I need to think things through."

Devastated, Echo opened the door and eased out.

After leaving Mariah, Echo decided to check on Faith since the last time she saw her she had a world-class attitude. But when she walked up to their building, she was shocked to see her sitting on the step holding her arm and Kari behind her consoling her. As if they'd been on the losing end of a brawl.

Heart pounding Echo rushed toward them and asked, "What the fuck happen?"

"Just go away!" Faith snapped, tears pouring from her eyes. "Go be with your fake ass friend and leave us alone! You don't give a fuck anyway!"

"Stop acting like a bitch and tell me what the fuck is up!" Echo yelled, shocking them both. "I'm sick of your mouth!" She stepped closer, not in the mood for anybody talking recklessly. "You gonna learn how to talk to me."

Faith rolled her eyes but remained silent.

"It's ma," Kari said softly. "She took our dresses to sell for drugs and jumped on Faith when she tried to fight back."

"What the fuck?" Echo yelled placing her hands on her face before dropping them at her sides. "She geeking that hard?"

"It's worse...I think she broke Faith's arm."

After the ambulance arrived to take Faith to the hospital Echo stormed into the house, angry at the world. Benita was sitting at the kitchen table looking at an apartment guide but Echo paid her zero attention. Concerned, on the way to her room Benita stopped her.

"We have to talk about our argument last week, Echo. I'm tired of you walking 'round here like you don't know me. And avoiding me. I'm your mother."

"I know, ma, I just want to go lay down."

Sensing something off Benita stood up and approached her. "What's going on?"

She sighed. "I don't want to talk about it."

"I don't care what you want to talk about! I'm asking you a fucking question!"

"Wanda just broke Faith's arm. She been abusing them for a minute and I'm tired of being quiet. They come to school with gashes on their bodies and I once saw a burn on Kari's leg. They too afraid to tell anybody because they don't want Wanda getting locked up."

"I'm not surprised," Benita admitted sitting down.

Echo walked up to the table. Frowning she asked, "You knew?"

"I didn't know about the abuse...but Wanda been going down hill for a while. Them drugs taking what's left of her senses I guess."

Benita knew Wanda didn't take the best care of her daughters but she never imagined abuse. Benita saw Wanda hanging with local drug abusers in the neighborhood, which is why she provided Kari and Faith with regular meals as much as possible.

She was a crackhead now but life wasn't always bad for Wanda. In high school, Benita, Wanda and her sister Kim were close. This was before Wanda's husband was killed in a car accident, resulting in her falling heavy into drugs and getting raped by a man in a crack house, resulting in Faith being born.

In the past Wanda valued Benita's opinion but now she felt that if she got into her business they would be enemies. But what could she do? She had information about two girls she loved being abused and she wouldn't be able to live with herself without stepping in.

She decided to deal with the details later but approach Wanda at once, whether old friends or foes.

Benita rehearsed silently what she was going to say to Wanda as she stomped down the street. Even though Benita was comfortable butting into her business, she felt a smooth intrusion would be best. Besides, the matter could get violent since children were involved.

As Benita approached Wanda's building, she checked to make sure her pocketknife was still secured in her jeans.

It was.

Ready to get down to business Benita knocked on Wanda's door hard. As she waited in the hallway, she couldn't believe the foul odor permeating from the apartment...even with the door shut.

"Who is it?" Wanda yelled, her voice heavy with 'tude.

"It's Benita." She said.

Wanda opened the door. "Thought you were my meddling sister. She always feels the need to get in my business." When she realized she said too much she cleared her throat. "Anyway what you want? Your girls not here."

"Can I talk to you in private?" Benita said. "Won't take but a minute?"

Sensing something was off she asked, "Do I have a choice?"

"I'll make this quick."

Wanda sighed and opened the door wider. As Benita walked deeper inside, she searched for a place to sit down. After the strong possibility that she might leave with roaches occurred she elected to remain standing.

"If this is about Faith's arm she's fine," Wanda said. "Fell down is all."

"That shit happens to boys not girls."

"What do you want, Benita?"

"Wanda, what has become of you? You used to be better than this." she paused. "I know since Nat died your life been hard but it was a car accident. Don't let it kill you and your daughters in the process."

"Don't talk about Nat!" she yelled, pointing a dirty finger her way. "He was the best thing that ever happened to me. You don't know shit about Nat." Wanda started crying.

"You right. I didn't know Nat well. But I do know he would want you to take better care of those children. I also know that he wasn't the best thing that happened to you, your girls are."

"What I do with my children is none of your fucking business!" she paused. "Now what the fuck do you want?"

Benita frowned. "Wanda, are you abusing those girls? Because I'm hearing things I don't like. Now if you need a break I'm more than willing to take them off your hands for a few days. I'm just a phone call away, you know that."

"Oh, I'm sorry...I didn't get the book you read."

Confused she asked, "What book?"

"The book that tells you when and where to discipline a child. Or the book that told you to walk your uppity narrow ass over here to get into my business."

Angry, Benita went off. "You know what...you's about a dumb ass bitch! You didn't get those books because you was too busy reading up on how to give head in an alley for crack!" She was so livid she was sweating. "The bottom line is this...everybody in this neighborhood takes care of those girls but you. So I have more of a right than you do to be in your business! I'm the one who feeds them children! You might as well call me daddy!"

Wanda giggled. "What I find funny is how you digging into my business when your daughter's a dyke!" she laughed. "You should be glad I even let my girls play with her."

Benita stepped back. "What the fuck you talking about?"

"Just like everybody in my business they're in yours too, sweetie bear! Believe that! Just today a neighbor saw your daughter and Mariah kissing in the basement. Feeling all up on each other like a man would a woman! So believe me when I say your sheets not clean either, sugar."

Silence.

"I'm going to have to ask you to leave!" Wanda continued.

Stunned, Benita quickly exited the apartment. Her chest felt heavy and the embarrassment made her skin hot to the touch. Here she came to read Wanda and had gotten her own ass handed to her instead.

The moment she was out the door she ran into Kim, Wanda's sister. Although heartbroken about the news of her daughter being gay she decided to try once more to save the girls. "I know its been a long time since you've seen me and normally I don't butt into folks business, but if you love your nieces you need to get them the hell out of there. Or spend your time planning their funerals."

She stomped away, leaving Kim furious.

CHAPTER FIVE
NOT ENOUGH MONEY IN THE WORLD

Echo stood in front of the high school waiting on Taja to come outside. Although she wasn't a fighter the last thing she wanted was her sister being jumped by a bunch of girls again. And since she saw her ignore Aspen and Harper in the hallway earlier in school, after they tried to talk to her twice, Echo figured she would be walking home alone.

She was getting irritated when suddenly Nasir pulled up in his new silver BMW with his mother Angela in the passenger seat. "Hey, Echo," he said leaning further back than necessary. "What you 'bout to do?"

She waved non-chalantly and turned back around, causing Nasir to pout like a spoiled brat.

"Echo, why don't you like Nasir?" Angela asked softly. "He'd do almost anything for you if you'd ask."

"He's cool, I guess." She shrugged. "I'm just waiting for my sister."

"I'll give you a ride if you want," he said excitedly.

"I'm good, Nasir." She smiled, not really wanting to hurt his feelings. "I appreciate it though."

"I can wait for your sister too if—"

Frustrated she moved closer to the car to keep shit real. "Listen, you're really nice," Echo said cutting him off. "But I'm not interested okay?" She was firm. "I'm sorry if I hurt your feelings."

She walked away.

Angry, he pulled off with his mother rubbing his back to console him.

"They weird as shit," she said to herself when they were out of sight.

After five minutes Taja finally came outside, looked at Echo and rolled her eyes as she walked away. Echo kept up the pace until she turned around. "I know what you doing but I don't need nobody looking out for me. So bounce."

"I'm just going home, Taja. And it just so happens that we live together so stop tripping."

"Let me make this clearer, I don't like you. I don't fuck with you and I want to be left alone. The only thing we share is blood and since you a dyke I'm not even sure about that." She stepped closer. "Now if you want to be stupid and still run behind me then that's on you but don't be mad if I swing on you."

"And you'll get dropped too," Echo said standing taller. With clenched fists she said, "Go ahead, Taja. You talking that fly shit so jump." She cracked her knuckles. "I'm begging you."

In that moment she was certain that the blackmail power she had over Echo was wearing off and she was afraid. "Like I said, leave me alone." Taja stormed away and Echo gave her space.

Fifteen minutes later she was halfway home, doing her best to keep her distance from her younger sister. She realized in that moment avoiding her was never because she was afraid of Taja, but she was afraid of herself, and what she might be liable to do if she snapped.

When she walked past a small wooded area she turned around when she heard whistling. The moment she did she was staring into the eyes of

Harper and Aspen. "Please, God. Make them keep their distance. I'm not in the mood today."

She felt her prayers fell on deaf ears when Harper stepped in her face and smiled. Her sweaty skin glistened and her flesh smelled like rank bologna. "What's up, Echo? Walking alone?"

"Yeah...funny seeing you here," Aspen added as she brushed Echo's shoulder.

Echo shook her head and moved around them but they blocked her path again. "Stay out my way."

"Why, in a hurry?" Aspen asked. "It ain't like you have a friend or a life. Might as well kick it with us for a little while."

"I'm warning ya'll...stay the fuck away." She paused. "I'm not gonna say it again."

"Wow...now she's tough," Harper laughed. "Since when did that happen because I didn't get the memo? Last I checked you were still a bitch."

When Echo tried to walk around them again Harper hit her on the top of the head with a bat Echo didn't know she had. Before she knew it both of them kicked and punched her so many times she was numb to the pain.

Although a few cars drove by, not one of them stopped and helped. Instead they shook their heads and went about their lives like what they were witnessing was normal. As they continued to pummel her she said a prayer to herself realizing it was all about to be over. "God, if this is how I'm going out I hope you forgive me for my sins. I never wanted to be like this...all I wanted to be was me."

Feeling lightheaded, she closed her eyes and gave it all up. Through the slits of her eyelids she saw a black Civic pull up and a large muscular driver exit quickly for the melee. "Get the fuck out of here!" he screamed at them. "What the fuck are you doing to this girl?"

Seeing the huge strange man coming their way, Harper and Aspen took off running.

Looking down at Echo he asked, "Are you okay, young lady?"

Silence.

"Maybe I should get you to a hospital." He examined her bloody body.

"No...please don't," Echo yelled. She rolled over, and sat on her knees for a second before he helped her to her feet. "Can you take me home?" she held her stomach. "I just want to go home."

A few days later Echo was sitting at the table with her mother and sister eating dinner. Over the past couple of days both her and Taja came home with bruises and cuts, neither giving a whole lot of explanation as to why. Benita was starting to learn that although she was their caregiver, as teenagers they were growing into their own right, evident by their more independent attitudes.

The meal was halfway over when Benita decided to break silence. "We're moving...to Texas." She looked at both of them. "I found a job there."

Taja's eyes widened and she came to the realization that her world as she knew it was over. Since she wasn't talking to Mariah, Echo could care less. "Why, mama?"

"Ain't a whole lot of money out here, that's why. And I got kids who eat and need clothing.

I'm only doing what I have to, to take care of my family."

"But I don't want to go," Taja rebutted. "I want to stay here with my friends."

"Even if I could let you why would I?" she looked at her and then Echo. "For the past week both of you been coming in here like you're at the losing end of a boxing match." She paused. "What's going on out there?"

Echo grabbed her fork and continued to eat her meal, without responding, doing nothing but pissing Benita off more. "Answer me got damn it!" she yelled.

Echo sat the fork down, looked at Taja and back at Benita. "I don't feel like talking about it no more because it don't make a difference anyway. You gonna go along with your show so just do it." She picked her fork back up and continued with her meal, astonishing them both by her attitude. It was one thing for Taja to act out from time to time but Echo had always been so passive.

Benita pushed the chair back and rushed over to her. She was about to strike her when the look in Echo's eyes told her it wouldn't be a good idea.

"I don't mean to disrespect, ma. But I got a right to keep my personal business just that...personal. I hope you understand."

Benita's stance remained planted as she frowned down at her. "Does this have anything to do with that girl I heard you were fuckin' in the laundry room?" she placed her hands on her hips and the look in Echo's eyes told her the information she received from Wanda was correct.

Echo stood up and looked dead into her eyes. "Who I choose to fuck is my business ain't it?" she smirked. "What I want to know is why you ran another man off again? Warren was the only one who could take your shit and you coming at me about a bitch? Please take care of your own before you check for mine."

Any other day she would never serve Benita so fully but her patience was as thin as water. Done with her mother, done with her sister, she felt herself heating up at the surface.

Taja gasped and Benita felt as if she'd been gut punched. She answered her oldest daughter's rebellion by slapping her so hard her body turned to the right.

Slowly Echo rolled her head until she was staring directly back in her eyes. Instead of exhibiting anger she laughed at her mother and walked to her room, slamming the door so loud three pictures fell off the wall and crashed to the floor.

The next day Echo was in her room, her things stuffed in several duffle bags by the door. Yesterday she decided she was done with it all, but especially her mother and would leave without explanation. Since Benita was at work she knew by the time she discovered she bounced she'd be long gone.

When the bedroom door opened Taja walked inside and saw Echo's belongings. "I found out why I got into that fight last week." She looked into the closet and saw all of Echo's things gone. "Harper told the main girl I said her mother was on drugs, so they jumped me."

"Who told you?"

"Mariah," she said softly. "Harper was mad that I told her she would never get married and planted a lie." Taja shook her head. "Dumb shit."

Echo shrugged. "Those are your friends."

Looking down at the bags again she said, "What's going on? Why you rolling out?"

Echo sat on the bed. "Does it matter?"

Taja walked deeper inside and sat on the windowsill. Looking out at the city she sighed deeply and turned to face her older sister. "I'm sorry...for my part in this shit."

Echo stood up and walked to the drawer to grab the money she tucked from the lunch she saved over the months. Although she didn't know it would be used to fund her escape, she was glad she kept it. "I don't feel like talking, Taja. So get the fuck out of here."

"I don't care if you accept my apology or not...even if you leave this room it won't change how I feel," she said harshly. "Like I said I'm sorry for not treating you like a sister."

She had Echo's attention. "Why didn't you?"

"I don't know...guess I didn't respect you. Hated you for not being the oldest sister I could come to."

"That shit sound dumb," Echo said waving her off.

"I also blamed you for daddy leaving," Taja said softly, revealing the real reason. "Before he moved to New York I overheard him telling mama that no daughter of his would be a dyke. Said if she didn't put you out, then he would leave."

"Put me out?" Echo's breath was heavy. "I was only twelve when daddy bounced." She paused. "How did he know before I did? I don't dress like a boy...or move like one."

By T. Styles   77

"Something about catching you being in the bathroom at the same time with one of our friends, looking at her coody cat or something. I think it was Faith. Not really sure."

"If I was I wasn't doing anything." Echo's feelings were hurt but she knew she had to move on. "Why you telling me this shit now?" She picked up one of the bags and tossed it over her shoulder, before doing the same with the other.

"Because I might never see you again."

"You know what...for too long I've been worried about what other people thought of me." She exhaled. "I don't even know if that will change anytime soon. I just know that I'm gonna go someplace else to figure it out."

"Well what you want me to tell ma?"

"Tell her I'm not her punching bag no more. Tell her if it bothers her to have a gay daughter now she don't have to worry 'bout it."

When there was a knock they both rushed to the living room. When Echo opened the front door she was surprised to see two black policemen. "Yes?"

Taja walked behind her.

"Do either of you know an Aspen Symons?" Officer One asked thumbs stuffed in his gun belt with authority.

Taja stepped beside Echo. "I do...She's my friend."

"She was murdered last night, looked like someone pushed her down the steps and raped her." Police Officer Two responded. "We need to ask you a few questions. Is your mother home?"

Echo sat outside on the steps in front of her building waiting for her cab to arrive. When Mariah pulled up instead and parked at the curb she started to go back inside and wait from the apartment. But Taja was an emotional wreck after learning that one of her friends was murdered and she needed air.

The police received reports that Aspen and Harper assaulted Echo and since Aspen was dead, they wondered if Echo was involved. Especially since she claimed to not know any details about the driver who gave her a ride on the same day they jumped her, which was also the day of the murder.

Mariah sat next to her on the stairs. "Heard about Aspen?"

Echo looked past her. "Yeah…"

"Didn't like her much…or her sister. But I wouldn't wish this on my worst enemy." She looked at her bags. "Where you going?"

Echo avoided eye contact, afraid that her feelings for Mariah would change her mind. "I don't know."

"So first Kari and Faith move with their aunt and now this? Come on, Echo. Don't do shit out of anger."

"Shit happens."

Mariah nodded in agreement. "Got any money?"

"Enough…"

Mariah dug in her purse, pulled out forty bills equaling four thousand dollars. "Take this." She placed it in the palm of her hand. "Lonzo gave it to me earlier to buy upgrades for my car. I can get some more later."

Echo examined the money.

She started to give it back but realized she needed it. Stuffing it inside her pocket she said, "I'll pay you back every dime."

"I don't want the cash back, Echo. I want our friendship. And I want things to be normal, like it was before we kissed."

Echo laughed and shook her head. "Why you keep talking about a friendship that never existed? Once you played with my pussy we had a relationship that you weren't willing to acknowledge because it didn't look how you wanted it. 'Cause I don't have a dick."

Mariah's stomach buckled. "So you cut me off?"

"Look, I'm 'bout to leave and I'm not coming back. You can change that, Mariah." She held her hand. "All you have to do is give me a reason to stay. Tell me you love me like I love you...and leave Lonzo alone."

The cab pulled up in front of the building as Echo waited for an answer.

Mariah looked at the driver and back at Echo. She eased her hand from hers and said, "Write me...."

Echo exhaled, stood up and looked down at Mariah. "There will never be another person who loves you as much as I do. You'll have a hard life trying to figure it out, but you'll find out soon enough." She walked to the cab and it pulled off.

"Are you gonna get out or not?" the cab driver asked rudely, looking at Echo through the rearview mirror. They'd driven for thirty minutes in circles, finally stopping at a particular address.

Echo looked out the window at the modest house on the outskirts of Washington DC. "I'm ready...how much I owe?"

He glanced at the fair although he knew the price when they stopped five minutes ago. "Thirty five dollars."

Echo reached in her bag and peeled off the money before sliding out the car.

Slowly she trudged toward the house and when she was ready she knocked on the door. Within seconds he opened it with a wide smile on his face that seemed to hide whoever he truly was.

"Hi, Nasir..."

"Echo...I'm so glad you came," he said softly, a goofy smile plastered on his face. "Come in."

CHAPTER SIX
EVIL HERO

"I like you in that...your body...it's so feminine," Nasir said as he gazed at Echo who stood in front of him wearing a red form fitting dress. "Why are you so perfect?"

Echo glanced down at herself. Her budding breasts, her curving hips and her newly manicured red toes which sat in a pair of Prada pumps. Everything she wore he bought...at the moment, even her soul. With all that said she looked like a million bucks.

"Do you like yourself?" he asked, talking like a man ten years his senior. He sat on the edge of his California king size bed and looked upon her as if she were his newest possession.

Nasir Case, son of two drug dealing parents by way of New York, who recently himself got into the game, wanted one thing above all...Echo Kelly. Prior to her showing up at his house he resigned to the fact that it would never happen. Until she called and said she'd run away and needed a place to stay. He quickly jumped at the chance to save her, convincing his parents if they didn't agree to allow her to move in he might never speak to them again.

Spoiled beyond reason, it was often easy to ignore his pampered behavior because he was so handsome. His dark chocolate skin and honey brown eyes gave you the impression that he was harmless but a closer glance would show you something else.

How did a teenager with so little time on earth already have access to everything his heart desired? And even more what kind of man did it make him never to hear the word no?

"I like how I look," she said softly. "More than anything I like that you like it."

He didn't seem pleased. "Echo, why are you *really* here? It's been three weeks and when I look at you, and talk to you, it's as if you tell me the things I want to hear. Like you're humoring me. Are you?"

"You helped me when I needed you. For that I want you to have everything you want, even someone who talks, looks and moves like you would like her to."

"But when I touch your body you cringe."

"I never had sex, Nasir. I just need a little more time if that's what you mean."

"Are you sure? That you've never had sex?"

She stared at him as if she were emotionally bankrupt. "What do you mean? Why would I even lie about something like that?"

He stood up. "You will never love me the way I want...will you?"

Silence.

"Probably not, but you won't feel the difference, Nasir. For now can that be enough?"

He violently rolled his shoulders as if he were uncomfortable in his clothes. Obviously holding back from acting out barbarically, he suddenly calmed down. "Take the dress off."

"Now?" she asked, thinking he wanted sex.

"Don't worry, I'll never rape you or make you do something you don't want. If you want me you gotta ask." He paused. "Take the dress off so you won't ruin it. You'll look beautiful in it at the party."

She removed the dress, and slid into her tight jeans, which put her ass back on bubble status. "Do you think it's a good idea for me to roll? Since I'm not in school anymore?"

"I want to show you off." He paused. "It's important for everyone to know—"

"You got the girl you always wanted," she said finishing his sentence.

He laughed.

"How come I get the impression that you have a date in mind?"

She slid her t-shirt on. "A date for what?"

"For when you'll leave me." He stepped closer and pulled her into his arms. "I waited a long time for this shit and I want it to last."

"Then enjoy the moment."

He frowned. Digging into his pocket he held something in his palm. Walking away from her he sat on the edge of the bed. "Ever wonder why I made you get your license within a week of moving here?"

"Not really." She shrugged.

He opened his palm and revealed a black key with the Mercedes Benz logo embedded within it. "I bought you something nice...it's sitting on the curb." He cleared his throat. "Well...my peoples bought something nice for you anyway. I just told her what I wanted."

Echo's eyes widened. "You bought me a car?"

"Now you smile." He grinned. "It's not a new joint but you'll still look pretty in it." He paused. "Come here, Echo." She walked over to him and he raised her shirt, kissing her on the belly button before placing the key in her palm. "Go...have fun and come back to me soon."

The cream seats in her blue C Class Mercedes groaned as she cruised down the block. Although Nasir owned a BMW, she appreciated the upgrade on her life even if it was temporary.

Echo knew her time with Nasir was limited. She could hear the virtual clock ticking in her mind, reminding her that soon she would have to leave and to not get too comfortable. She didn't want him anyway. Besides ever since Mariah awakened her sexual desires, she found herself horny beyond belief.

Add to that her growing anger with having to be with a boy she didn't want. When he touched her, even for a hug, every fiber of her being shivered. It was like her skin was covered in a million tiny worms and she hated him for it.

Although Nasir was always available, he didn't have what she wanted. She needed...she desired...the feel of another woman. Her clit ached as she thought of the last time she was with Mariah and it seemed to stay with her always, like she was chasing a high.

Something else was happening.

Now that she didn't have to live with her mother she was growing more confident in who she was. No she wasn't prepared to claim lesbian-hood, but she felt bolder to go after what she wanted.

Bitches! And many of them.

Cruising down the streets, the smell of the new car permeating through the air, she saw a cute girl her speed sitting at the bus stop and pulled over. "Where you going?"

She looked around wondering whom Echo was talking too. Realizing it was her she said, "About ten blocks up. Why? You offering?"

Echo popped the locks and the girl ran over and hopped in the passenger's seat before she could change her mind. "What's your name?" Echo asked.

"Brittney...and yours?"

"E...my friends call me E."

She smiled. "I like that and since I plan to be a friend, hello E. I like your face even more."

Echo looked over at her. "Is that right?"

She nodded.

"You have pretty lips," Echo complimented as she continued to maneuver the car. "I want you to use them. You with that shit?"

Brittney's jaw dropped before getting herself together. Seductively she said, "Why we wasting time? Pull over."

Echo tucked her car behind a building, away from prying eyes, and pushed her seat backward. When comfortable she eased her jeans down to her ankles, along with her pretty red thongs and placed her honey colored thigh on the driver's console.

Brittney wasted no time diving in.

Her warm tongue circled Echo's clit like she'd done it many times and she realized Britney was not just a cute face, but a pro. What she found awkward was that she must've unconsciously known that she was "in the life" which is why she pulled over.

How else could she hit the jackpot?

Palming the back of her head Echo didn't let it go until she exploded her cream all over her lips.

Lipstick Dom

When she was done Echo pulled her clothes back up and checked her face in the rearview mirror.

Horny...Britney excitedly opened her legs and pushed her seat back, expecting Echo to return the favor. But when Echo pulled off without another word she was shocked. "So you gonna do me like that? Leave me hanging with a wet pussy?"

Silence.

"Excuse me...are you gonna say something?" Britney continued with an attitude. "Or just keep driving and shit?" She was so mad her light skin was flushed.

"You gonna tell me where I'm dropping you off or do you wanna get out right here?" Echo looked over at her and waited. "It's your call."

"To be fem you act just like a nigga, bitch."

Echo shook her head and laughed. "Whatever you say, but I got mine and don't give a fuck."

"Nasir, what's wrong, son? Are you and your cousin fighting again?" Angela asked gazing at him across the kitchen table. Her sagging facial muscles were polished with expensive makeup. "I hate seeing you this way, please talk to me."

He looked at the clock on the wall behind her. "Have you ever wanted a thing bad? And when you get it, it's not what you expected?"

She smiled and wiped her mouth with a white napkin with pearl colored trimming. "When I first met your father he didn't love me. He cared about me, but it wasn't love." She forked some spaghetti and placed it between her thin lips. "At first I thought it would always be that way but I knew in my heart he was the one for me."

"What did you do to make him change his mind?" he positioned himself so he could hear clearly.

"I waited, patiently, as he went through woman after woman. Like a fool I allowed him to look for something else but I had a plan. It was clear. I would become the woman of his dreams. Disguised as a friend I learned the things that moved him and became his everything and he wanted for nothing. I was perfect and never gave up. In the end, when the smoke was clear, he realized that I was everything he needed. A few months later he made me his wife."

Nasir looked down at his plate. "But what if...what if..."

"The girl is gay, Nasir." She ate some more. "At least she thinks she is." She wiped the corners of her mouth. "Before we do anything you have to understand that."

He sat back in his seat, confused. "It doesn't make any sense. She's not butch or nothing. I mean how do you know for sure?"

"Benita told me in confidence one day. Figured if she met you she'd change."

His body slumped forward. Then what do I do?" he paused. "Let her go?"

She slammed a fist down on the table and everything rattled. "Have I ever raised you to walk away from what's rightfully yours?"

"No..."

"Then don't start now."

"So what do I do?"

"You know, by bringing that girl into our home I had to give up Benita's friendship. She would die if she knew the daughter she was searching for was in my house." she paused. "But I didn't mind putting everything on the line because I want my son to know the world is his."

"I know...and I thank you. And dad."

"That's not gonna be enough, son. She needs a lesson in gratitude. Your father had to set me right a few times and it worked. My bones healed before long and everything."

Frowning he said, "I don't understand."

"Give her something to feel, Nasir. Make it hard because she's a tough one." She smiled. "Trust me when I say...she'll hear you then."

Echo was on her knees in the backyard of Nasir's house, tucking money and jewelry inside a shoebox she hid behind the shed, within a few feet of dirt. When she was done she brushed her knees off and stood up, only to see Nasir standing in front of her.

"You don't have to hide the things I give you." He reached in his pocket and extended a thousand dollars. "Here...put this with the rest."

Echo's heartbeat thumped wildly.

She'd been caught planning for her escape.

She accepted the money and with the same hand he yanked her forward and punched her in the face, breaking her nose. Her mouth filled up with blood as she fell backwards, banging her head into the shed.

Echo was starting to think she made a mistake but how could she leave?

She thought about her long lost friend.

Mariah was willing to do what she had to, to take care of herself. Whether it be dating a man she didn't love or letting her father rape her, she moved forward. But after Nasir put his hands on her she came to the conclusion that Mariah's path was not hers.

Sitting at a stoplight she placed both hands on the steering wheel of her brand new car. When the light turned green she slammed down on the accelerator, going even faster. Instead of taking the curve necessary to make a right, suddenly the large oak tree in a yard looked appealing.

Pressing the gas to its limit she rolled up on the curb and slammed into the oak tree. The windows shattered and the car caught on fire.

Realizing the crash was just a bad dream she popped up in bed and wiped the sweat off her brow. "If he don't kill me I'm gonna kill myself. I have to get out of here."

A few days after Nasir hit her, Echo packed her clothes quickly within the darkness of his room. Walking around the house with two black eyes and a bandaged nose, she couldn't believe her life

Lipstick Dom

had come to this. Maybe it was a bad idea to leave home after all.

She had to escape.

It was now or never.

Luckily Nasir was with his parents visiting an aunt at the hospital and she knew if she didn't leave immediately he would eventually end her life.

With both duffle bags over her shoulders she was about to exit the house when Nasir walked through the front door. He was as calm as a summer day.

In fear, Echo froze in place.

"Don't worry...I'm not gonna stop you," he said as he sat on the sofa. His attitude was relaxed and nonchalant, scaring her even more.

"Where are your parents?" she asked, jaw trembling, hoping they would protect her.

"They stayed with my aunt." He leaned back in the sofa and sighed. "I don't know why...but hospitals always put me in a bad mood." He smiled. "Well what are you waiting on? You can go."

She was just about to take him up on his offer when he said, "Oh...did you hear about what happened to Mariah? I know ya'll not cool anymore but I had to tell you."

Echo froze and looked at him.

"Relax...it's nothing bad. She's single now," he smiled.

She shivered. "Why you...why you mentioning her name?"

"Well...if you won't be with me I'm thinking about fucking with her." His chest poked out. "And hard too. Outside of Lonzo ain't another nigga in DC our age that can afford that type bitch. Except her own father."

There was tightness in her expression. "Leave her alone, Nasir! I'm not fucking with you!"

He threw his hands up in the air and they flopped in his lap. "If you walk out you won't leave me no other choice. It's either her or you. What's it gonna be?"

Echo stared into his eyes, knowing he was serious. She dropped her bags.

Grinning he said, "You know, it's a shame I have to do so much to get your attention." He walked over to her and stepped in her breathing space. "When we gonna stop fighting?"

Tears rolled down her face. "You turning me into something else, Nasir." She paused. "And I don't like how it feels."

"I know," he said wiping her tears. "And I'm sorry but you made me wait so long. I feel like if you gave me a chance you'd see that I'm everything you want. Everything you need. I can make you happy, Echo. I mean look at what my parents are doing for you. They letting my bitch stay in the crib. Bought you a car and everything. Why can't you act right? Why can't you be more appreciative?"

"If I stay you can't hit me anymore...ever."

"Then don't give me a reason."

Her teeth gritted. "How did you know?" She skipped the subject. "That Mariah broke up with him?"

He frowned. "Who said anything about breaking up? The nigga Lonzo dead."

Echo's eyes were closed tightly as she lie in the bed with Nasir. She was doing her best to appear sleep as he spooned her from the back, his warm chest pressing against her flesh.

Needless to say she was irritated beyond belief.

Several nights ago after learning that Mariah had suffered the loss of her boyfriend, Echo's first instinct was to contact her and restart her friendship obligations. Besides she was certain that Nasir had him murdered. But when she called home, and spoke to Taja during the hours she knew her mother wouldn't be home, she decided not to after hearing what she had to say.

"Basically she hates you," Taja said plainly. "Something about you leaving and now she can't trust anybody."

"So I'm to blame for her boyfriend being killed?" Echo said as she whispered into the phone. No one was home but she couldn't take the risk of Nasir morphing up behind her as usual.

"You know it ain't 'bout blame, Echo. It's about her moving through her pain alone. Outside of Faith and Kari you were all she had I guess. With them gone who's gonna be there? Her father? Or her mother who's too miserable to be any good?"

Echo sighed. "Don't talk to me about that nigga Rick. Ever. Somebody should've wasted his ass too." She was about to tell Taja everything but she held back.

"Wow...not sure what that's about but okay."

She wanted nothing more than to reach out and to tell Mariah how much she loved her. But shit was different since the rejection. It was bad enough her mother didn't accept her sexuality, the last thing she needed was Mariah playing on her weaknesses by blaming her for not being there.

"I need you to look after her," Echo said seriously. "She going through a lot at home and needs support."

"You know I don't fuck with that girl like that."

"Do it for me, Taja. You said you were sorry for how you carried things before I left. Prove it."

"I'm not playing into that shit," Taja paused. "Not for blackmail reasons anyway."

Echo smiled. "But you will do it though right? I'm begging you."

"To tell you the truth me and Mariah have gotten closer since Aspen was killed and you left. In this neighborhood I guess we the only ones with sense left. So yes, I got her back."

"Thank you..." she paused. "So how's ma?"

"Bad...really bad. I had to tell her that I heard from you so she could sleep at night and stop calling the police. Now she seems to be mad about you running away and not reaching out."

"So basically she's back to normal..."

"Pretty much." She laughed. "But look, I'll keep up with Mariah as long as you don't tell them..."

"Tell who what?"

Playing, Taja hung up the phone, forcing a laugh from Echo she hadn't given up in awhile. "That girl crazy as shit," she said to herself.

With Mariah taken care of now it was time to handle Nasir and Echo knew just how to do it. If he wanted to put his hands on her and force her into his personal prison she was going to put him out of his misery.

So as he snuggled up behind her, she could feel the cool handle of the knife she had tucked under her pillow. When she was ready she was going to bring it across his neck, severing all his major veins.

But first she had to seduce.

So she moaned a little and wiggled her ass against his penis. They hadn't fucked but she was willing to give him the illusion that she was ready.

"You playing games?" he said softly. "Or are you serious?" She could feel his heart beat against her back as he anticipated a yes.

"I wouldn't play with you, Nasir. I finally get that you own me. And I'm tired of the silent treatment. You're right, we need to stop fighting."

"You don't know how good it feels to hear you say that." He rolled her body over so that she could look down into his eyes. Her arms were raised above her head, with her hand on the knife tucked under the pillow. If he knocked the pillow to the side he would see the shiny blade easily.

Luckily for Echo he didn't.

"I'm happy you feel good...that's all I want." She opened her legs as if inviting him inside. She hoped he wouldn't enter her before she had a chance to kill him. But she was willing to give him a shot of pussy if necessary.

Pushing her legs further apart he gripped at his penis. Just when he was about to plod inside, she knocked the pillow off, raised the knife and pressed the blade against his neck. Upon seeing the shimmer of the weapon against his brown skin he swallowed the lump in his throat.

"So you gonna do me like this?" his voice quivered. "Kill me in my mama's house?"

"I never fucked with you. Even when I moved here I only wanted what you could give me. But now you want to bring other people in the picture. People who have nothing to do with this shit? You won't get Mariah, I promise you that!"

"Echo, I would never—" Instead of completing his sentence he stole her in the face so hard that the knife plopped out of her hand.

Crawling over top of her he hit her repeatedly as the flesh of her face opened under each blow. She could feel herself getting lightheaded as he continued to take his anger out on her. Things were getting dark when suddenly she managed enough strength to push him off of her weakening body.

On his way down to the floor, he hit the side of his head against the edge of the dresser. Ready to fight for her life Echo leapt off the bed, grabbed the knife and straddled him.

He was out cold.

She was just about to slash his throat when Angela opened the door after having heard the commotion. Wearing a long red silk gown she looked like she was ready for her movie close up. "Please don't!" she yelled, hands quivering in the air. "Please...don't take my son away from me."

"Stay right there!" Echo yelled, barely able to see through the slits of her swollen eyes. "I'm not fucking around! I'll kill this mothafucka!"

Angela froze in place.

Examining Echo's bloody face she said, "I'm sorry for whatever just happened here. But he's my only son." Huge tears rolled down her cheeks. "And I don't want to live without him. Please, Echo...don't do it."

"Where's your husband?" she asked looking around her, afraid he would enter with a gun.

"He's not here," she said calmly. "It's just you, me and Nasir. And all I want to know is if there's a number that I can give to make this situation go away. Any number at all."

"Why do you think you can buy everybody?"

"I'm sorry...you're right...and I know he can be a handful but it's not his fault it's mine. If he's fucked up I'm to blame."

Echo glanced down at him. He was still out cold as she took in his mother's words. "So you're the reason he's like this? You're the reason he thinks he can beat women?"

Guiltily she said, "I raised him...so I have to say yes."

Echo looked down at him. "I won't take his life."

Angela exhaled in relief.

"But he will never have any children. Not in this lifetime." She raised the knife and aimed for his penis.

PART TWO

Lipstick Dom

CHAPTER SEVEN
PRESENT DAY

Karen crept slowly toward the red Acura, with the sounds of her shoes clacking softly against the pavement. When she made it to the car and looked down at the dark windows she realized she couldn't see inside. She didn't know if it was fear or the tint that hindered her view.

Either way her heart was rocking.

She was just about to turn around and call the police when the passenger door flew open and a beautiful woman holding a gun aimed at her stepped out. "Get in the backseat, bitch!"

"Please, don't shoot," she said with raised arms. "I was just coming to see if anybody needed—"

"Get the fuck in the car!" the Passenger screamed. "I won't ask you again."

Karen quickly opened the door and eased inside the Acura. Once she was inside, the passenger sat in the backseat with the gun still trained in her direction. Karen glanced at the driver's seat and noticed that the woman sitting there was dead. Her head was drooped to the right and blood flowed down her shoulder and onto the carpet.

"Who are you?" the passenger asked. "Why are you over here?"

Trembling she said, "I was just...I was just..."

"Getting in business that has nothing to do with you." Her gaze bounced around, as if she would shoot at any minute.

Karen nodded. "I'm so sorry. If you let me leave I won't say anything."

The passenger's stance was stiff. "I can't trust you."

"I promise!" Karen pleaded, doing her best to sound confident. "I'll get in my car and go home. And you'll never hear from me again just please don't kill me."

"I don't know you. Even if I wanted to believe you I can't take the risk." she glanced at the corpse. "I knew her for years and I thought I could trust her too." She glanced back at Karen and cocked the weapon. "Look at how she ended up."

Karen began to cry hysterically until the butt of the weapon came crashing down on her forehead, silencing her instantly. "No fucking crying," she yelled.

Karen covered her mouth with both hands.

"I need silence," the passenger continued with wild eyes gazing around the car. "I need peace until I can figure all this shit out." She looked deeply into her eyes. "And if you knew me, you'd do well to heed my warning."

CHAPTER EIGHT
15 YEARS LATER
LIPSTICK DOM

As Echo allowed the water from the showerhead to run over her body, she was trying to rid herself of another broken heart—a broken heart not her own.

She knew she had to face Sapphire the moment she stepped out of the shower and because of it she wanted to prolong the soothing stimulation as long as possible.

Echo's home was elegant.

She had every luxury available to a drug dealer...dark color schemes, Jacuzzi tubs, chandeliers.

As Echo wiped the soap from her face, she thought more about Sapphire who was lying horny in her bed. She dated plenty of women since realizing she loved pussy and they all wanted the same thing...a relationship.

Echo on the other hand desired excitement. Although she loved the smoothness of Sapphire's body, she wanted nothing more. Freedom and space was priority. The last and only woman she ever loved was Mariah, whom she hadn't seen in fifteen years.

"So I'm face up in bed, pussy tingling and body warm and soft," Sapphire yelled from the bedroom. "Are you gonna come out here and finish me? Or do I have to do it myself? Again." she cooed. "Echo!" she moaned. "Where are you?"

Echo dried off, opened the bathroom and said, "You gotta bounce."

Sapphire looked at Echo's body. It was sculpted to perfection...long legs, phat ass, small waist, medium sized breasts and a beautiful face. Sexy by default, she switched into the bedroom and sat on the edge of the bed. Removing the Chanel No 5 scented lotion from her nightstand she rubbed it over her legs.

"Did you hear what I said?" Echo asked seriously. "I have a lot to do tonight and you not a part of the plans. Remember?"

"What's more important than me and you right now?"

Echo looked down at Sapphire's light brown skin and her short hair cut that looked cute in any style. Physically she was boss's wife material, mentally she was a basket case who could fuck in the bedroom and cling to the person long after the sex was over.

"You really want me to answer that and hurt your feelings?" Echo asked.

"Humor me."

"I told you Faith is being released from prison today. I gotta get shit prepped at my club." She paused. "Even invited you but you didn't want to roll."

Sapphire's skin seemed to redden with anger. "Because I wanted to chill with you...alone. Anyway what she do to get locked up? Whenever I ask you act like it's a big secret."

Echo sighed. "She murdered Aspen, a childhood enemy."

"Why?"

"Not sure really." Echo ran her hand along the side of Sapphire's face. "Get different reasons every time I ask. But when her and her sister were coming up they went through a lot of shit in the neighborhood. Aspen was one of the main perpetrators. I guess after awhile you get tired of eating shit."

"Is that why you were locked up?"

Echo laughed. "What is this? Twenty one questions?"

"Since you're in the talking mood, which you never are, I'm trying my hand."

"I got locked up for almost cutting off a nigga's dick. Cut off his thumb when he woke up instead."

Sapphire laughed. "The ultimate dyke."

Although she thought it was funny, to Echo it wasn't a joke. She spent five years in prison for attempting to kill Nasir. But she was smart and learned a lot behind bars. She learned how to conceal her emotions to prevent her enemies from getting wind of her premeditated actions. She also mastered the art of moving dope, courtesy of white boy Ryan, a dude she dealt with who wrote her after seeing her on a Prison Pen Pal site. He saw her pretty face and felt whatever she was in jail for wasn't warranted.

Big mistake.

Echo was a star chameleon, telling him everything he wanted to hear during their five-hour weekly visits. He kept money on her books making her powerful behind bars. When she was released he rescued her. Knowing it was time to let go of her virginity for the betterment of her causes, she fucked him so good he thought he was black.

Playing the dutiful wife, she also pretended to be meek and submissive as she looked over his shoulder during the times he cut coke, cooked it and picked up his paper. Quietly she breathed in each detail, not missing a thing. And when she was ready, she popped five bullets into his torso and took his stash. Later tucking his body in the river like money in an off shore account, with the help of her best friend Six, a dominant lesbian who proved more loyal in prison and outside than anybody she ever met.

To her delight the day Echo was unleashed from prison Six was also, and they'd been getting money together ever since.

After the coke she stole from Ryan was moved she got up with Bambi Kennedy, one of the Pretty Kings— a ruthless drug quartet who were as beautiful as they were deadly. Since Bambi had a thing for putting women in powerful positions, she set Echo up with the proper packages and her empire was born.

Although Echo was getting money with Six by her side, she was always worried if Nasir would reemerge. After slicing his finger he moved away with his parents and nobody saw him again. She was so concerned that he would come back for revenge that it used to keep her up at night. She had one slice and should've used it to take his life instead of his manhood.

"You playing but I'm about to throw your ass out of here in a second," Echo said.

"You mad?"

"I'm getting there."

"Well let's go another round. You always liked fucking when you have an attitude," Sapphire continued, as she removed the covers to reveal her voluptuous breasts. She widened her legs and said, "Now come get this pussy, bitch."

Echo chuckled.

Echo placed the lotion back on the nightstand and kicked off her slippers. Examining her sexy body she said, "Why do you make things hard?"

"Because I want you to think about me as much as I do you."

"And you think staying when I ask you to leave will work?"

Sapphire stood on her knees in the bed and massaged Echo's shoulders as her breasts rubbed against her back. "Echo, why do you throw me away?" Sapphire replied softly. "I love you and before you say anything I know it's not returned."

"Then why say it at all?" she asked, as her fingertips started to put her at ease. "I told you not to fall in love. I told you before I ever kissed that pussy. Dealing with me was a dangerous game, yet you played anyway."

"Everything about you is soft and feminine, but you have the mentality of a stud." She paused. "Why don't you want to fall in love?"

"Who needs love? It just complicates shit."

"Well...come here. Make love to me and I promise I will leave."

"You gonna leave if I fuck you or not." She paused. "But I'll play along.

Echo turned around and kissed her and she could taste the mint on Sapphire's tongue. Unwrapping her towel, she threw it on the floor and pressed her breasts firmly against Sapphire's.

A soft sigh escaped their lips.

With one hand Echo grabbed the sheet and using it as a cape, threw it over her shoulders. Slowly she covered Sapphire's body with her own. Placing a finger into the warmth of Sapphire's plushness she could feel herself moisten. "I see you kept it nice and wet for me."

"Whenever I'm around you it's the same," she moaned.

The tightness of her pussy and her heavy breaths were intoxicating so Echo decided to let go. She crawled on top of Sapphire, maneuvering her body until their pussies kissed. With small circular motions and a lot of pressure, Echo moved as if she were fucking her with a dick, and in Sapphire's opinion it felt better.

"I love you," Sapphire breathed in her ear. "If only you'd give me a chance you'd see I'm the one for you."

Echo kissed her cheek and ran her tongue alongside her neck as Sapphire clawed at her back. Sapphire's body convulsed before settling into tiny tremors.

Echo was the best she'd ever been with. Fifteen years of sexing women on a regular meant she was no longer a rookie in the bedroom. She was willing to do whatever it took to please her partners, taking in every inch of their bodies until she knew them better then their doctor.

"Open your legs a little wider...I need to hit that shit right."

When Sapphire complied, Echo grabbed Sapphire's waist and pressed down firmly over her pussy while gliding on top of her juicy clit. "I'm about to cum, Echo. Oh my god!"

"Let me hear you..." Echo demanded.

Suddenly Echo felt a tingling sensation come over herself and sensed Sapphire was on the verge of a climax too. Placing her lips over Sapphire's she gently suckled her bottom lip. Before reaching ecstasy she felt Sapphire's body quiver, realizing she was about to be satisfied.

No longer able to hold back, Echo felt a warm sensation creep up her spine and take over her body. She placed Sapphire's succulent nipple in her mouth and pressed her clit firmly over hers again.

Echo was cumming.

It was a wrap.

When Sapphire tried to reposition herself, almost fucking up the groove, Echo grabbed her closely and controlled the situation. Don't move," Echo demanded. "Not there yet."

Sapphire remained still and warm as Echo got hers off. The session was so proper Echo thought about chilling for an hour since everything at the party was taken care of until Sapphire said, "If I had it my way I'd kidnap you. Make you stay all night."

Echo climbed out the pussy. "Well you don't." She stood up. "So get the fuck up." She slapped her thigh. "Before I throw your pretty ass out."

CHAPTER NINE
ECHO THE GREAT

Echo was tucked in the back of a white Porsche limo as it made it's way to her latest venture— *Echo's Dame Strip Club*. Six of her bodyguards were also present— all of them taller than her 5'7 inch frame, and wider than her voluptuous body.

If they were walking behind, on the side of her and in front of her, you couldn't see her in the middle. They were beyond loyal because Echo took care of them and their families, and as a result each one of them laid their lives on the line for her.

Looking like the drug lord she was, the soft glow from the starlight ceiling shined on her diamond chain with the cross that sat right above her ample cleavage. Dressed in a form fitting business suit, no shirt or bra, Echo looked sexier than the dames who danced for her.

"Don't fuck none of our bitches, Six," Echo said firmly, adjusting the diamond cufflinks on her jacket.

Six flashed her award-winning smile that had all the bitches geeking. Rubbing her short natural curly mane, her hand dropped in her crouch as she leaned back. She was cooler and finer than the average nigga. "You know I wouldn't fuck none of the—"

"I'm not playing with your red ass, Six. You can't be getting the girls all mixed up where they can't work and shit. We done fucked some of the baddest bitches...but the ones in here are off limit. Don't forget, you promised."

Six adjusted the white gold chain on her neck and wiped invisible dirt off her black Versace tee. "Aight, man. You ain't gotta keep telling me shit I already know." She pulled her gun out, checked the clip and crammed it back on her waist.

"Why you carrying? That's what we got them for," she said pointing to the bodyguards who touched the hidden weapons on their hips.

"I move around too much. They cute and everything but they protecting you."

Echo laughed knowing she was telling the truth.

"Can you believe this shit?" Six said when she gazed out of the window and saw a line around the club. "All this to see a little pussy?"

"We handpicked fifty of the baddest bitches. Had 'em trained professionally and everything. Niggas respect that shit and don't mind spending money."

"You mean *I* handpicked them," Six laughed. "All you did was have me give 'em those long ass applications. Like they in the secret service and shit. We almost couldn't find enough girls to meet your qualifications."

"We got a lot of money running in and out this spot. We need to make sure the clientele here is safe, and that means no shiesty bitches. Them long ass apps gonna come in handy one day. Mark my words."

When the limo stopped Echo whispered to Arnold to be on the lookout. He was her most trusted goon and she relied on him for almost everything. Afterwards the bodyguards slid out and surrounded Echo and Six as they glided toward the entrance. It was a long time coming to reach the level of success Echo had obtained but it was well worth it.

By T. Styles 109

Although the money was good, the drug dealer lifestyle was coming to an end for her. The plan was to get the club up and running and in six months she would be done. Out of the game for good.

As they moved, people attempted to take pictures of Echo but it would be in vain. In Echo's opinion if someone could take a clear picture she was too open to snipers so the circle was always tight.

Once inside the club she was impressed and hoped Faith would be too when she saw the decorations. Everything was beautiful, just as she envisioned. Dark lights...expensive blood colored furniture accented in gold. And of course the vodka waterfall pouring over huge crystal letters that read, 'Welcome Home Faith'.

The moment Six saw the girls dancing in their VIP section, as if beckoning her, she said, "Uh...I'll wait for you in the trenches." She broke through the bodyguard circle and high tailed it to VIP before Echo could respond.

All Echo could do was laugh.

"It's about time you got here," Kari said approaching Echo.

Kari kept in contact with Echo over the years, often visiting her in prison also. Their friendship grew stronger once Echo saw how loyal she was, and when she got home she did well by Kari financially. Especially since Kari had a dead end job as a nurse, at a facility that paid her cheaply. Echo needed trusted people and wasted no time offering her enough money to quit and work for the club.

The rest was their history.

"Taja just called and said she picked up my sister at 5:00 this evening, took her to the Ritz

Carlton and got her dressed in the outfit you bought. She should be here any minute. But I have to talk to you about something right quick..."

Although Echo heard some of what was said, she thought she was seeing things. But when she blinked a few times she realized her vision was correct.

Nasir was sitting in her spot smiling her way.

Looking at Arnold she said, "Kill that mothafucka with the grin on his face!"

"Oh my, God, Echo please wait!" Kari said stopping him and the rest of Echo's men. "That's what I'm trying to tell you. Mariah's here too!" she paused. "She's with him."

Before Echo had a chance to completely understand she saw Mariah looking like a million bucks in her establishment. The white silk strapless dress with white designer pumps and Chanel clutch bag told Echo Mariah was well kept, as usual.

Still, Echo and her guards moved toward them. Her men kept hands hovered over their waists in the event Echo wanted them to light Nasir up.

Echo's heart rate increased and when Mariah stepped forward and tried to touch her Echo's men pushed her backwards causing Nasir and his two goons to leap forward.

Bad move.

"Echo, please!" Mariah begged.

Echo's guards raised their weapons and it looked as if there was about to be serious gunplay on opening night until Echo pulled herself together and told her men to relax. Knowing what she meant they lowered their weapons and Nasir's men followed suit.

"How did they get guns in my club?" Echo asked Kari.

"I'm sorry, I didn't know they were strapped when I brought them in," she responded. "I mean, they were with Mariah and I thought shit was cool."

Breathing heavily Echo asked, "What are you doing here, Mariah?" She also looked at Nasir.

"I'm here for Faith," Mariah said, softly. "And her coming home party." She looked at Kari. "Didn't you tell her you invited me? I told you she would be mad."

Echo glanced at Kari who said, "You didn't give me a chance to tell you when you came in, Echo. You wouldn't answer your cell phone either."

Echo was so deep in Sapphire's pussy she avoided the call. Her temple pulsated as she focused on Nasir, still not understanding the correlation. Why were they together? It was because of Mariah she sliced the nigga when he threatened to hook up with and beat her as he did Echo.

And then she remembered, she didn't tell anybody but Sapphire what she'd done. And that was only recently. Shame caused her to hide the fact that she almost went medieval when he abused her.

So how could Mariah know?

"This is my husband," Mariah smiled.

Echo glanced down at Nasir's hand; he was still missing a thumb. The same one that protected his penis that he almost lost. "You married this clown ass mothafucka?"

"You know...you look like a female but talk like a nigga," Nasir said slyly. "What I tell you about that mouth? Didn't I school you on it behind the shed at my crib? You need another lesson?"

Mariah was confused. He'd always told her that nothing happened between them. And since Echo was hoarding her by not talking to her, she couldn't get more information.

Echo appeared un-fazed as she walked up to him and smiled. Everyone in the room was stiff wondering what was about to happen. As quickly as flipping a light switch, she gripped his dick, bringing him to his knees.

And when his men tried to get famous her goons surrounded them, relieved them of their weapons, and lifted them off their feet with neck holds.

"Never forget, talking to me sideways almost lost you this." She squeezed harder, causing the vein in the middle of his forehead to pulsate as sweat puddles rolled down his face. When she saw the manhood being drained from him, she released the hold.

Wiping her hand on his shirt she stepped back. "I don't fuck with you...and you know it. Should've never showed up at my spot."

Nasir wanted to rip her throat out but knew it would be far from possible. She rolled too deep and at the moment his men were in a bind.

With one knee on the floor he said, "You should've never did that."

"You threatening me?" she asked harder than any nigga behind her.

Suddenly Six hopped over the velvet rope sectioning off VIP and stood at her friend's side. She was in the bathroom and missed everything.

By T. Styles   113

"Aye, Echo? What's good?" she asked, nostrils flaring. Her words may have been kind but the manner in which she delivered them wasn't. She quickly scanned her surroundings looking for the culprit of Echo's dismay.

Since Echo never told Six about Nasir, Six was clueless on what upset her so much.

"It's fine, Six," Kari said trying to diffuse the situation. "The nigga already got his nuts squashed. Let's not go too far."

Six looked her way. "Not for nothing, Kari, but I'm not talking to you." Focusing back on Echo she said, "You aight?"

Echo blinked a few times. "Yeah...I'm good." She paused. "This an old friend." She pointed at Mariah. "But this is an enemy." She looked down at Nasir. Gazing at her goons she said "Let them go." They released Nasir's men who were finally able to breathe.

She was about to give orders to give Nasir and Mariah the rough road out when Mariah grabbed Echo's hand, melting her anger momentarily. "Can I talk to you for a moment?" she paused. "In private?"

Silence.

Finally Echo nodded to her men that it was cool.

Two men followed them to her office while the rest of the guards stayed with Nasir and his men. The tension was so thick in the club it made the large establishment feel smaller.

When they were behind closed doors Echo sat on the edge of her desk as Mariah observed her boss steez. She couldn't believe how beautiful she'd gotten after all of these years.

She was model like with killer style and extremely sexy.

Slowly Mariah approached unsure of how to come at Echo. She was aware of the friend she loved as a kid but this person seemed to be different. "I missed you," Mariah said softly.

Echo shook her head. "That's why you called me back here? To reminisce?"

Echo's harsh tone crushed her feelings. "I can't believe after all this time you still hate me."

Echo stood up and walked toward her chair, with Mariah catching a glimpse of her plump ass. When Echo was seated she crossed her legs. "Why would you fuck that nigga? He a clown. I mean did you fall off that hard where you gotta mess with punks?"

"What?" Mariah's jaw dropped.

"Answer the question."

"Echo, I don't see how this—"

"Either answer it or don't."

Mariah sighed. "Because I love him, I guess. And if you must know we have a decent sex life."

"You playing yourself with that dude. But it ain't my business."

"If it ain't your business why you so mad? I thought you didn't like him? And he told me ya'll were never together so what's the problem?"

"The nigga don't want you, Mariah. He's only with you to get at me."

Mariah frowned. "That was arrogant."

"That was truth...and one day you gonna find out."

"But why are things so serious between you two?" she paused. "The last I heard you were into women."

"Let's just say you bedding my enemy...and that makes you my enemy too." She looked deeply into her eyes. "Is that what you want?"

Not knowing the deadly legacy that Echo had built, she invaded her space by moving closer. A wiser person, one who was familiar with the hierarchy in the streets, would've known that this move was a no-no. Standing next to her she said, "What I want is communication with you. We're not kids anymore, and I get it. But can we at least be friends?"

"You too close," Echo said calmly. "Back the fuck up."

Mariah froze in place and moved away.

"I'm not the same girl you played mental games with on the block." She reached in the drawer and separated four stacks of cash. She tossed it to Mariah and she caught it. "That's the four thousand dollars you lent me plus interest."

Mariah frowned. "I don't want this."

"Then make it rain on the bitches out there."

Mariah blinked a few times and her body slumped forward.

"You want anything else?" Echo asked.

"No...I..."

Echo stood up and switched toward the door. She stopped in front of Mariah and said, "I'm serious...Nasir is only with you to get at me. Ask him. See if his eyes tell you the truth."

The party was in full fledge mode when Faith finally arrived.

Echo saw to it that not only her gear was fashionable and in style, but that she was given fifty thousand dollars to start a new life. If Echo had money it meant her friends had too and that was the bottom line.

Two hours into the celebration and Faith, Kari and even Taja, were drunk and throwing ones and five dollars over the women as if they fucked bitches. Six disappeared about an hour before with a cute little chocolate girl with a fat ass.

Echo was another story.

After Mariah pleaded with Echo for fifteen minutes, she agreed to allow Mariah and Nasir to chill. His men were thrown out on the streets. She hoped at the very least that would cause Nasir to leave, but he acted like he could care less either way.

All night she tried to enjoy herself but her attention was occupied on what Mariah and Nasir were doing. Something didn't feel right and when she thought about it more she believed that her feelings were involved. She would have to get over it. They were married and the way Mariah was talking she appeared to be happy.

Needing a bit of fresh air Echo walked toward a side door, stealing the attention from all of the strippers on the dance floor due to her cold body and boss personality. When her men tried to follow she stopped them abruptly before walking out the door.

Mariah, seeing this, rushed behind her.

Catching up with her on the side of the building, Mariah grabbed Echo by the hand. Echo pressed her against the side of the brick wall, grabbed a fistful of her hair and yanked it sideways before gazing into her eyes.

Despite being in pain Mariah didn't pull away.

For ten seconds the women who, before this moment weren't on speaking terms, were kissing passionately. "You want to play this game? Where we fuck behind your husband's back?" she paused and snaked her fingers under Mariah's dress and into her panties. "If you do you'll be my little secret. Is that what you want?"

Mariah hearing her own words felt gut punched. "Echo, I'm...confused."

"You're not confused, Mariah. You're gay." She laughed. "I'll play the game but on my terms." She paused. "Now get out of my face."

Mariah straightened herself up and eased back inside the club.

Echo walked toward the limo and without saying goodbye to the rest of her friends, she ordered the driver to pull off.

Having seen the kiss with Echo and Mariah, Sapphire sat in an old black beat up Hyundai she owned that no one knew about. She used it to sneakily follow people without their knowledge. And because it was a far cry from her cherry red Escalade, she always got away with it.

Behind a foggy window, Sapphire slowly lost what was left of her mind. "I hate you, bitch!" She yelled, mascara running down her face. She looked like a mad woman. Although Mariah had been long gone she was giving her the business. "You can't have her! Do you hear me? You can't fucking have her!"

After slapping the steering wheel several times she eased out of the car, stomped barefoot toward Nasir's 7 series BMW, and flattened all but one of the tires.

CHAPTER TEN
CRAZED SEX SLAVE

After driving around for an hour, the limo finally pulled up to Sapphire's house...a modest brick home in Alexandria Virginia.

Echo didn't want to be there but the night was still young, so she commissioned a little company.

Within seconds Sapphire stepped out, hips swiveling toward the vehicle. Her red lips smiled as she ran her hands down her hips, which was covered in a very form fitting dress.

Once the door opened the mint she constantly wore eased inside with her. "Echo," she said seductively.

Echo's eyes rolled from her painted toes to her blood red lips. "Sapphire..."

The driver pulled off.

"You know, when I saw your name on my caller ID my pussy tingled. I was sure I wouldn't hear from you tonight...with Faith's party and all."

"You never know with me," Echo said, rubbing the side of her face. "I'm an enigma."

"You look sad."

"My mind is busy," she winked. "But I'm here."

"What happened at the party?"

"Mariah was there. The girl—"

"I know who that bitch is!" She said with wild rotating eyes. "The only female you ever loved."

Echo smiled. "Didn't realize I told you about her."

"It was in the beginning," she responded, consumed with jealousy.

"Well don't worry about it, she'll be in my circle because we have the same friends but she's married now. No need for you to get all riled up."

"Is that so?" Sapphire said grinning. "How do you feel about that?"

Echo looked into her eyes. Running her hand down her face she squeezed her chin softly. "I'm not here for talk...let me feel your lips."

"Your wish is my command." Sapphire wiggled between her legs and slid down Echo's slacks. "Has anybody ever given you head in a limo?"

"You want the truth or a lie?"

"It doesn't matter, because this is going to be as good as it gets," she winked.

Within seconds Echo felt Sapphire prying her cream La Perle panties to the side as she snaked her tongue into her wetness. Up and down around and around Sapphire licked every inch of Echo's pussy until no spot was left untouched. She went at Echo's clit as if her life depended on it. As the driver continued down the street she focused specifically on Echo's button using small circular motions.

Echo was done.

She grabbed Sapphire's head and opened her legs wider. She could feel her hot breath and wondered if this was how it felt to have your dick sucked. "Keep...it...just...like...that." Echo bit down on her bottom lip savoring each moment. "Keep sucking that shit, beautiful."

With one more tongue flip Echo's orgasm seemed endless. To be sure she was satisfied Sapphire lapped up her juices softly, raised her head and smiled. Her lips sparkled.

By T. Styles   121

As usual she was thoroughly impressed with Sapphire's oral skills.

Echo closed her legs, raised her hips and slipped back on her panties and slacks.

Sapphire took a seat next to her and licked her lips. "When are you gonna realize that when all the other bitches are dead and gone, that I'll still be here?"

Suddenly Echo was blown.

"Sapphire...I'm feeling you. The moment I got a girlfriend position available you in there, but right now I'm doing the single life. Can you get with that? Or do I have to keep having this conversation with you everyday?"

Sapphire looked out the window, her body slumping.

"Why you sad?" Echo asked.

Sapphire turned around and looked at her. "That's my pussy, Echo. I stamped that shit. And you should know any bitch that tries to get in the way of that, including your precious Mariah, will get dealt with."

The next morning Echo woke up and walked down to her kitchen. Her chef prepared an assortment of breakfast selections for her and Sapphire but her heart was heavy and because of it her appetite was lost. Not only because Mariah being back around brought up memories, but also because she hadn't spoken to one particular person in years.

After Echo ran away from home, and got locked up as a juvenile, she unknowingly foiled her mother's plans to move to Texas, something Taja was appreciative for. While searching for Echo in the beginning she lost her job and had to remain in DC once she was found.

Having gotten the number from Taja earlier in the week, Echo picked up the phone and dialed every digit, making sure to block her number. "Mama..."

"Echo...is that you?" Benita asked excitedly.

Echo smiled at her enthusiasm. "Yes...how are you?"

"Living. Making ends meet."

Echo frowned. "You been getting the money I sent you right?"

"Every cent."

Echo sat down and exhaled. "So what you do with it? Bought a nice house?"

"No...I gave it away to the church. Figured they could use it more than me."

Echo's head dropped. "Mama, I send you fifteen thousand dollars a month. You giving it all to church? Why? That money is for you."

"It's drug money, Echo. And I don't get with drug money, you know that. Add to it my daughter being a..."

"Lesbian."

"Dyke," Benita shot back. "That's what you are aren't you?"

A tear ran down Echo's face and she was angry with herself. It had been a long time since she cried and she didn't miss it one bit.

"And then you had the nerve to open a spot where women dance around naked." Benita paused. "Had the people talking about it at church and everything. You even got your sister lying for you, trying to say the club not yours. What have you become? I didn't raise you like that!"

"I know you hate me but I'm still your blood. No matter what, I will always love you."

"As long as you eat pussy you ain't no daughter of mine. Never call me again."

Echo hung the phone up and ran her hand down her face.

"Ms. Kelly, can I prepare you a plate?" the chef asked.

"No...I'm fine." Echo stood up and walked out.

Sapphire, who stood in a small bathroom off the kitchen, heard the whole conversation. She picked back up the phone and hit redial. Disguising her voice she said, "Ms. Kelly please." She pressed her lips against the phone so that no one could hear but Benita.

"This is she."

"So this the black bitch who would deny her own daughter. This the bitch who be trying to act like she didn't fuck a bitch or two back in the day." She laughed. "You ain't nothing but a hypocrite."

"What are you talking about?" she yelled.

"You think people didn't know you and Katie were licking each other's pussies?" she laughed. "Imagine my surprise when I found out your so called best friend was the biggest dyke in D.C."

"You don't know shit about me!"

"Bitch, I looked up the T on your ass. And while you sitting over their judging, make sure bones not falling out your dyke closet."

Click.

Sapphire hung up.

"Who were you talking to?" Echo asked walking up behind her.

Sapphire's face turned red and she felt like she was about to shit on herself. "Just...just...one of my friends."

Echo kissed her lips. "Well come on...it's time to eat."

Relieved she said, "I'm ready when you are, baby."

CHAPTER ELEVEN
TWIN LIVES

"Barry, I don't know where Faith is," Kari said as she smeared mayonnaise on her ham sandwich in the kitchen. "Call her back in a couple of hours."

"I think it's fucked up I held shawty down in prison and now she home acting brand new." He paused. "I mean what I do wrong?"

Kari rolled her eyes, knowing full well Echo was the real contender for Faith in jail, dropping thousands. Barry was the clingy type of nigga that didn't give you breathing room and she could see why her sister was turned off. Faith met him in high school, right before she was arrested and he'd been hooked ever since. Everybody knew about the blowjobs Faith delivered for money but Barry was the only one completely sold. The moment his eyes rolled back he wanted to wife her and then she was arrested for murder.

The honeymoon was over too quickly for him.

"I don't think you did anything wrong." She licked the mayo off her finger and closed the jar. "She's been in prison half of her life. Give her time."

She could hear heavy breaths but the line went silent before the call ended all together.

"Wait...did this nigga just hang up on me?" She placed the handset down. "Fuck his black ass."

The truth was, Kari didn't know what was going on with Faith. Lately she'd been distant and although they shared an apartment together they barely saw each other.

Things were going smooth in Faith and Barry's relationship until *he* walked in the picture. His name was Donte Maxwell— standing 6 feet tall he was all muscle, most of it being dick. Since Faith was on light skin men hard, hating her own complexion most of her life, the last thing she wanted was to stay with a man with skin like hers.

That meant Barry didn't have a chance in hell.

Physically it was easy to see why Faith was attracted to Donte, but Kari could tell he was bad news just by the changes in Faith's mood. He had fast cars and fast money to go with it and with him she felt like a star.

So why was Faith always broke?

When she heard keys in the front door, she knew her sister was home and Echo's heavy laughter told her she wasn't alone.

"I know you love me, nigga," Faith said as she and Echo walked into the living room. "Look at how you brought me home. Bammas still talking about that party."

"Fuck that party. I can never find your ass," Echo said jokingly. "It's been two weeks and you keep standing me up for lunch. And why you look crazy? The dick that good you can't even comb your hair?" Echo placed her MCM on the couch and followed her into the kitchen. She hugged Kari when she saw her eating her sandwich.

"Look...I'm doing me," Faith responded. "Ease up because you playing me close."

"Speaking of finding your ass Barry just called again." Kari said. "And when I told him you weren't here he hung up on me."

"Fuck his fat ass," Faith said opening the refrigerator. "I'm on Donte these days." She took the limejuice out of the refrigerator, placed her crusty mouth on the spout, drank some and put it back.

Echo and Faith watched in disgust.

"Are you okay?" she asked.

"Damn, I wish ya'll just leave me the fuck alone already!" she yelled. "Just cause a bitch got a life outside of this clique don't mean nothing wrong."

"So why you so secretive these days?" Kari asked.

"Because you can't keep secrets." Faith said. "Maybe that's the reason I don't tell you shit."

"You sure about that? Because I never told Echo you were crushing on her in high school."

Faith wanted to shit herself when she heard those words and Echo was shocked. She may have had a chance if she took better care of herself but she never did. Faith was thick in the right places and her body was always in tact no matter how much she ate.

"You are so fucking ignorant," Faith said trying to skip the subject. "I just wish ya'll stay out of my business."

"What the fuck is wrong with you, son?" Echo said. "A rack of niggas don't have nobody to care about them. Be glad you have plenty."

"I hate to do this in front of Echo but she family," Kari said placing her sandwich on the bare counter.

"Well you already told Echo something I told you in confidence. So now what?"

"I don't think you've dealt with what happened to us. As kids."

"I'm about to go," Echo said sensing some drama was about to kick off. Whenever Wanda was a topic the situation never ended good.

"No...don't leave," Kari said. "You know about how we grew up."

Echo hopped on the counter and placed her hands in her lap.

"You kidding, right?" Faith asked, nose flaring. "I'm not dealing with what happened to us? You the one running around telling everybody how great that bitch was!" her body tensed up. "She was a monster, Kari! And you should start telling the truth! Deal with that!"

"She was still our mother." Her voice was low.

"Let's be clear...that bitch was *your* mother!" She moved closer. "And don't get in my face about her no more, okay? Do it one more time and I'll never talk to you again." She turned around to Echo. "You got some money I can borrow?"

"It's in my purse in the living room."

Faith walked out of the kitchen to get the cash. A few seconds passed and the front door closed.

She didn't even say goodbye.

Kari picked up the sandwich and tossed it in the trash. "You making shit worse by giving her money." She paused. "She spent that entire fifty grand in one week."

"I got it to give. And as long as I do she got it too. That goes for all my friends."

Kari shook her head. "I can't with Faith right now," she said waving her off. "Anyway, what's up with you and Mariah? Finally make amends?"

"Not really. She called a few times but it seems fake."

"How long you gonna make that girl suffer?"

"She married Nasir."

"You didn't like the nigga! Who cares?"

"I don't. I realize I'm over her."

"Is that why you fuck so many bitches? So you don't have to think about her?"

Echo opened the freezer and grabbed the vodka. "I fuck bitches because I like to fuck bitches. Nothing more, nothing less."

"You gotta be careful about who you bed. You act like you can't get enough sometimes. I mean must you and Six fuck a new one each week?"

"As long as I can still cum I'm gonna get off," she winked. "Anyway I'm coming over here to tell you to be careful when you out and about. I don't trust Nasir."

"When are you gonna tell me why you act like he's so dangerous? Seems real soft to me."

"Just do what I tell you. He has a grudge against me that he might take out on those I love."

"Then why you cool with Mariah being with him?"

"She been with the nigga for over a year. What could possibly happen now?"

"Please tell me you didn't have nothing to do with flattening his tires the night of the party." Kari looked at her. "Because that's young girl shit."

"I almost broke the nigga's neck." She frowned. "What I look like fucking with his car?"

"Well somebody did."

Echo shrugged. "The nigga got a lot of enemies." She paused. "If anything I think he the one who called my mama's house. I don't know what was said but Taja told me some bitch called and played on the phone. Had her all upset and shit."

"You think its Mariah?" Kari asked with wide eyes.

"I don't know what to think...just bet not find out."

"Whatever you say..." Kari lit fire under the teakettle. "I just don't know why you think it's cool to hurt a friend's feelings on purpose but if you ever cared about Mariah you would let the dumb shit go."

When Echo heard her cell phone ring she rushed toward it in the living room. It was sitting on the table.

Alone.

"Wait a minute...where the fuck is my purse?"

CHAPTER TWELVE
OBSSESSED

Nasir and Mariah were taking a soothing hot bath. Their tub was large enough to seat two people side by side but she was nestled between his legs, her back against his chest. "You fucked Echo before?" Nasir asked as he rubbed his four-fingered hand and thumb nub over her wet soapy breasts.

She turned her head and looked up at him. "Why would you ask me something like that?" she smiled. "That's my friend."

More intensely he said, "Have you fucked her or not?"

"No," she lied. Out of nervousness she searched for the washcloth and soap. "We were best friends at one time, but things changed. Got older I guess."

"Because if you did I wouldn't be upset."

Mariah sat up, turned around and looked at him. "Why not?" she paused. "If I'm your wife you should be upset if I slept with someone else."

"Not another bitch." He paused. "It's different. Anyway I want you to be happy. That's what marriage is about right? Happiness."

Silence.

"Mariah..." he said.

"I'm listening, Nasir. I was daydreaming for a minute I guess."

Nasir kissed Mariah on her forehead, violently grabbed her hair and pulled her toward him. With her hair tangled between his fingers, he looked down at her.

"Mariah, I'm going to need you to start paying more fucking attention to me!" He said in a serious tone. "I'm going to need you to start giving me some of the things I want in this marriage."

"Okay, baby," she smiled although she was horrified. "Whatever you want."

Since she'd been married to Nasir, there were many outbreaks where things ended violently. Once he broke her leg, another time he fractured her collarbone and there were more situations where he blackened her eyes. But Mariah felt she needed a man to take care of her, so she suffered through it all. Never telling a soul.

At first she was confused because she knew he liked aggressive sex in the bedroom, and to please him she always complied if he requested to tie her up or use objects to push in her body. But lately things had been getting worse.

Everything about their relationship was awkward. After Echo sliced him, almost severing his penis, he had his mother contact Mariah after hearing it was her birthday.

Sitting in a hospital recovering, he lavished her with expensive gifts, even giving her the Mercedes he bought Echo. But he never loved her, and didn't even like her for that matter. It was Echo he was after. He figured if he got Mariah's attention he would get Echo's too, and he was right.

But Mariah suffered extreme abuse because no matter what she did, she would never be Echo. And he beat her not because Echo didn't want him, but because Echo loved her so much.

"I'm sorry, Nasir." She touched the side of his face even though he hadn't released her hair. "Let's not argue tonight. Please."

"It's not about arguing," he said, gripping tighter. "Either you start giving me what I want or this is over. I ain't got a problem throwing you out on the street."

"And what do you want?"

"Convince Echo to let shit go between us..." He released her. "Do what you need to make that happen. I don't care what it is."

Mariah and Angela were getting their toes done at a salon in Washington DC. Every so often Mariah would stare at her intensely, driving Angela insane. "Say what's on your mind, girl," Angela said as she continued to read her Essence magazine. "You gonna have people thinking we a couple the way you keep looking over here."

Embarrassed, Mariah swallowed the lump in her throat. "Does your son love me? Does he ever talk about me at least?"

Angela smiled and shook her head. Placing the magazine down she said, "He still after that girl, huh?"

"Who? Echo?"

She nodded yes. "I think so, but I don't understand why," Mariah said. "She's not interested in him, never has been."

She sighed. "When he was in middle school he was hospitalized for mental illness. It seemed to come out of nowhere really. At the time Keith and me didn't know what went wrong. He was always so agitated no matter what you did for him and Keith was against medicine at the time." she paused. "But when he tried to jump off a bridge we had no choice...we had him committed.

"It was so sad, for two weeks he was in this place begging us to come home. He cut at his face, his legs and later his wrists. Nasir was miserable until a little girl named Wish Hawkins was brought into the facility." Angela smiled. "She was the prettiest little thing you ever did see, bright eyes, wide smile...and just as damaged. Before coming to the program she was abused by her caregivers...who beat and starved her because they claimed she ate too much. Stupid shit." She shook her head. "She was removed from the home but her mind was messed up forever." She paused. "Did he ever talk about her to you?"

"No...never," Mariah asked glued to her every word.

Angela reached in her purse, removed her phone and showed her. "This is a picture of her. When she first got to the home. I snapped the photo a few years ago when I found it in my house."

Mariah's jaw dropped. "She looks like Echo's little sister."

"Could be her twin...and I'm not sure that she isn't," she joked. "Anyway, he fell for her. Head over heels and believe it or not they both started getting better, until the accident."

Her expression tightened. "What accident?"

"At one point they were moved to a place in the clinic that wasn't so restrictive. It was for children on their way home. In that place there was a vending machine, where kids with money could buy snacks during meal hours. Well one night Wish wanted something...some type of chips I think. Nasir put the money into the machine but whatever he bought didn't come out. So she placed her hand in the slot...tried to pull it out. It still didn't work. Nasir got behind the machine and rocked it not thinking straight. The thing fell on her and she was killed instantly.

Mariah held her hands over her mouth. "Oh my, god."

"He never got over it. Blamed himself and was consumed with guilt. Afterwards he was worse off than when he went in. It took three years to get him back home and to a reasonable state of mind." She sighed. "Things were going good and then he met Echo...the spitting image of Wish." Her eyes teared up. "I don't think there's a thing he wouldn't do for her, but she hates him so much and it breaks my heart." She paused and looked at her as if she had the best idea ever. "Do you think you could talk to her? Get her to see the man he really can be?"

Mariah frowned. "I'm his wife, Angela. Why would I talk to another woman?"

Snapping back to reality she said, "Oh...you're right."

Mariah realized Echo was right when she said he didn't want her. But she also made a decision to never tell Echo, not wanting her to feel guilty for anything.

"My son needs you." She said coming to his senses. "And I have to tell you something. Sometimes...not all the time...he might get a little violent but he doesn't mean to be that way."

Mariah frowned. "Where did he get that from? That it's okay to beat women?"

Angela cleared her throat and skipped the subject. "Look...I know its hard hearing that your husband has problems, but hang in there. Soon he'll see what you mean to him. But whatever you do don't give up...I don't want my son to be alone, or chasing after a woman he can never have. It will set him back forever."

CHAPTER THIRTEEN
NEW KIND OF FRIENDS

"Can you get me a fake ID?" Mariah asked Echo as they sat outside on the restaurant patio at the National Harbor in Oxon Hill Maryland. The water sparkled and Echo felt uncomfortable because it wasn't a romantic dinner even though it looked like one. But since Mariah picked the place she let her live.

Echo's eyebrows rose and she smiled widely. "We haven't even finished our first round yet." She joked raising her glass in the air. "Already you hitting my head."

"I'm serious."

"Of course I can get you that. And whatever else you need." She paused, her tone a little more serious. "Is everything okay? Anybody hurting you? Because I can help with that too."

"No...it's nothing like that." She looked down at her fingers clasped in her lap. "I have my own reasons." She looked back at Echo. "So you're really all the way gay right? No men?"

"What the fuck is all the way gay?" Echo laughed, before crossing her legs. Several male callers came to the table trying to get their attention and her bodyguards pushed them all back.

"You know what I mean...just answer the question," she giggled, her cheek length bob moving every time.

"Yep...just women." Echo whipped her long hair over her shoulder. "I've always been gay and on this side nothing has changed but my age. But trust me...If I could turn it off, I would. I don't wish this life on nobody." She glanced at her phone and looked disappointed.

"No word from Faith yet?"

Echo shook her head no and stuffed the cell in her purse.

"What do you think is wrong with her? That would cause her to steal your purse?"

She sighed. "Remember when you tried to give her the dress for that party, and she caused a scene and walked away without taking it?"

"I think I do. But so much has happened in my life that things are starting to blur. Why you ask?"

"I think she did it because she doesn't think she deserves the best. She spent so much time taking shit that she can't accept when it's being given to her."

"You calling the police to report it?"

Echo frowned. "I don't snitch my friends out, especially for a purse I can have delivered in an hour. Faith knows I got the money, which is probably why she did it. What bothers me is her reason for stealing."

Mariah was suddenly uncomfortable. "You don't think she...you know..." she paused and picked up her fork to play around with her food. "Is using like her mom?"

Echo nodded. "I'm gonna give her the benefit of the doubt but it does look like she's using." She sighed. "I'm gonna rap to her in a couple of days, if I can get her to stop dodging me."

"I'm glad Wanda's dead." Mariah moved uneasily in her seat. "She put Kari and Faith through a lot of shit. And now this!"

"You telling me something I already know." Echo focused on Mariah and quickly looked away. She wasn't trying to get caught gazing, especially since she was making an attempt to keep things platonic.

After talking to Kari Echo realized it was stupid to put up fronts. Mariah was her friend, even if in her heart she always wanted more. It was better to remain cool, and be there for her in case Nasir flexed, or risk Mariah needing help and her never knowing. "Does he make you happy?" she paused. "Your husband?"

"We have problems like anybody else." Mariah shrugged. "At the end of the day I care about him and he cares about me."

Silence.

"Mariah...is he physical with you?" This time Echo was firm.

Mariah's eyes widened in disbelief. "What? No! Why would you even ask me something like that?"

"If we going to be friends I have to know everything about you. Even the stuff you don't want to tell me."

Mariah looked down at her glass of wine. "Why didn't you like him? Back in high school?"

"How could I like him when I was in love?"

Mariah's light skin blushed. "With who?"

"Let's not play games. I'm done with them."

She held her head down before looking up slowly. "He ever hit you, Echo?"

She laughed. "If he makes you happy, it doesn't matter."

"Are you happy?" she paused as she fidgeted with the linen tablecloth in her lap. "I know in the gay culture it's mostly about sex not love."

Echo was insulted. "Who told you that dumb shit?"

"I just know," she shrugged. "Every time you see a video where two women are laid up its for a man's sexual gratification. It's not about intimacy or a long term relationship."

"Mariah, that's not true and whoever told you that got shit fucked up."

"So answer the question...if it's not true are you in a relationship?" Mariah said already knowing the answer would be no.

Echo looked into her eyes and saw doubt. It was time to shock her. "Actually, I am. I've been with my girl for almost a year."

Mariah swallowed the lump in her throat.

"Oh...so who is she?"

"Her name is Sapphire. You'll meet her soon."

Mariah nodded. "I'm glad to hear that, Echo." Her voice quivered. "I really am. Because I worry about you sometimes."

"Why worry about me?" she grabbed her glass and took a sip. "I'm good. Really."

"Is that why you have six bodyguards hovered around us?"

Echo looked up at them. "That's just the nature of the beast." She paused. "They are around me everywhere so I forget they're there sometimes."

"You like it I love it." Mariah grinned. "You talked to your mother lately?"

"I have no words for that bitch and she has none for me." She paused, trying to hide her pain. "What about you?" Echo remembered the last time she saw Mariah's father and tried to appear un-fazed. She had nightmares to the day seeing her get raped by her own daddy. "You still cool with your pops?"

"He's still an active part of my life." She paused. "And I'll leave it like that." When her phone dinged in her lap she looked down at it. It was a text from Nasir.

Nasir: U talk 2 her yet? She with it?

Mariah: I haven't seen her. I'll let U know when I do.

She sent the message and looked back up at Echo. Smiling she said, "What were you saying again?"

After being treated like a second class citizen by Mariah Nasir called his daddy...

The cell phone was pressed against his ear as he sat in his car, looking over at Echo and Mariah at the restaurant.

"Son, what you're asking is impossible," Keith said angrily.

"But I need you to do this for me." His hand twitched as he held the steering wheel tightly. "You're my father."

"I know who I am and it doesn't matter!" he yelled. "When Echo did what she did...to you...I asked then what you wanted done. We had eyes on her in the prison and could've had her killed then but you said no. Said you had a plan of your own." he paused. "So what you do? Allow her to get out and become big enough in the game, where killing her is no longer an option. Don't you understand? With the clout Echo has its impossible to touch her without causing problems with peers. Son, you're gonna have to let it go."

Nasir's nostrils flared. "You said you could do anything."

"I can...but I won't jeopardize the business that has given you every luxury known to man. Your mother has allowed you to get away with enough as is. And on another day you know there's nothing I wouldn't do for you. But it's time to stop this. Let...her...go."

Nasir squinted as he continued to eye them. "Don't worry, I'll take care of it myself."

"No you will not! I am not about to get into a drug war because your feelings are hurt. I can't believe I'm having this conversation again! You're married, son! Do you remember the shit I did at your request so you could obtain that pretty wife of yours? It took years to convince people that Lonzo was killed by some New York niggas instead of the drive by shooting I orchestrated. Now, make the best of your situation and leave the matter alone!" he paused. "I'm warning you."

Nasir ended the call and made another. "Itch, it's me. Nas."

"What's good?" he yawned. "I was just about to hit you."

"Remember that thing we talked about last week?" he focused on his wife and Echo laughing happily at the restaurant. "Well make it happen."

"I'm on it!"

CHAPTER FOURTEEN
ANYTHING BUT MY HEART

Echo strutted into her home, only to see Sapphire standing in the middle of the room wearing nothing. Although she gave her permission to stay over, she almost forgot.

Seductively Sapphire stood directly in front of Echo. With her breasts exposed, she switched closer and wrapped her arms around her waist. "I have decided that I'm going to make you love me, Ms. Kelly." She kissed her lips. "And just so you know, my ring size is 7.5, which means I'll be wifey."

Echo grinned. "What I tell you about pushing it?" she slapped her ass causing her cheek to jiggle.

"There's not another bitch who's gonna be down for you more than me. All I want you to do is realize it."

Echo thought about Mariah moving on with her life.

Could she be right?

"Now you know I've heard that before right?" Echo asked.

"Yes, but I want you to remember this moment so when it finally happens, I can say I told you so."

Echo laughed and walked to the sofa. "Come here, sexy," she demanded grabbing her hand and pulling her closer. "But get on your knees and crawl."

Sapphire reduced her height.

"Turn around."

Sapphire adjusted her body, so that her belly was resting on the cool glass coffee table.

Slowly her ass rose in the air and her pinkness opened up.

Echo's clit tingled as she took in her body. Slowly she eased her index finger into her center. "Squeeze," Echo demanded.

Sapphire tightened the muscle of her pelvic floor and her pussy gripped her finger, causing Echo to smile. "Good girl...now sit on the floor and open your legs."

Sapphire turned around. "I thought I was relieving your stress, Ms. Kelly."

"You are," she winked.

Sapphire eased on the floor and slowly opened her legs.

"Now make it shine," Echo demanded wanting her to play with her own pussy.

Sapphire placed her index finger on her clitoris and slowly rubbed it in tiny circles. When it started feeling really good she flipped her button up and down, applying a little more pressure. Within minutes her pussy was so wet it sparkled like a diamond.

Just what Echo ordered.

Loving her submission Echo scooted closer to get a better view. "Damn, baby." She parted her lips and kissed her throbbing clit softly, causing Sapphire to moan.

"I love you so much, Echo," she whispered, her body practically convulsing as she bucked her hips.

"I know you do," she responded.

Without warning Echo slipped her tongue in and out of Sapphire's moistness. Her opening was tight, as a woman who wasn't fucking men should be.

Unable to hold back, Echo grabbed her legs and engulfed her pussy more firmly.

Sapphire shivered and wiggled around the floor; unable to take the way her she tingled. But Echo controlled the situation by holding her tightly and within seconds she exploded on her lips. "Damn you tasted good."

Horny as shit, Echo came out of her jeans and red lace panties. Slowly she crawled her slick box on top of Sapphire's. She maneuvered her hips back and forth, rubbing her clit on top of hers.

With one arm wrapped behind Sapphire's neck, and the other gripping her waist, Echo was in complete control. Whispering in Sapphire's ear she said, "I'm about to make you mine. If I do don't fuck up, you won't get another chance."

"I won't," she said as she wrapped her arms around Echo's waist. "If you give me a chance I swear to God I won't." She wanted her so badly she felt like she could cry.

Echo continued to glide on her pussy until Sapphire stopped her. "Please sit on the couch...I want you to cum in my mouth."

Echo eased on top of the sofa, and Sapphire dropped to her knees. Her head fell backwards as she enjoyed Sapphire's warm tongue slide against every inch of the wetness she helped create. She was in awe at how Sapphire always managed to find her spot....*quickly.*

"Right there, sexy," Echo said softly. "Get ready...I'm almost there." Seconds later Echo exploded into her mouth, biting her lip so hard she almost drew her own blood.

Sapphire continued to lick her pussy until it was dry and when she raised her head Echo was holding a key.

Sapphire wiped her mouth and with wide eyes asked, "Is that...is that?"

"I want you to move in and be my...be my..."

"Woman?" she asked hopefully.

"I wouldn't have it any other way."

Sapphire stood up, straddled Echo, looked down at her and kissed her sloppily. All the while Echo wondered if she hadn't just made a mistake.

The thing was...now it was too late.

Echo was in bed with Sapphire when her cell phone rang on the nightstand. Thinking it was Arnold calling about business she grabbed it and shot up. Quickly she pulled open the drawer and snatched another cell that she used for important orders, which needed to be delivered to her men if something was wrong with the blocks.

Slowly she walked naked toward the bathroom as if she had all the time in the world to take the call. Finally she said, "Hello." She leaned against the cool wall, leaving the lights out so her eyes wouldn't throb.

"Did my wife tell you I was sorry about how I treated you when we were together? Because I asked her to."

She looked at the phone. "Hold up, who the fuck is this?" Echo asked, believing she was hearing things.

"It's Nasir. And if you and my wife gonna be friends again it's important that we cool too." He paused. "And before you say the wrong thing, understand that I have more power than you realize right now. Please be nice and make the right decision."

Half sleep Echo wiped her eyes with her fingertips before her hand dropped. "Where is Mariah?" she yawned. "Because I know she doesn't know you're calling me."

"In my bed...where she belongs."

"Word?" She laughed softly. "You want to see real power?"

"What does that mean?"

"Answer the question, nigga."

Thinking she was still the girl he knew in high school he said, "Sure...I have time."

Suddenly all of the phones in Nasir's house started to ring. With one text message from her bat line she exhibited real power. The cell phone he was talking to her on rang— even the three he had in various places around the house— all went off. But it was the knock at the front door that had his little heart shook.

"What did you just do?" he asked, half of his confidence down the drain.

"Answer the door, Nasir," she said calmly.

"Why?" he yelled. "So you can...so you can have a nigga shoot me?"

"If I wanted you dead you'd be done already." She paused. "I saw you lurking at the harbor. Could've had your brains blown out then." She laughed. "Now open the fucking door."

Nasir grabbed his gun under the kitchen sink and walked to the door. Before complying he looked out of the peephole, cocked his weapon and pulled it open.

Arnold was standing there with a box of donuts. On some ridiculous shit he opened the lid and said, "Want one?"

When Nasir glanced inside he saw that half of the dozen was missing. What he didn't know was that he'd been sitting outside of his house all night.

"What the fuck is this?" Nasir asked.

Arnold smiled at him and walked off.

Nasir watched him the entire time as he bopped to his car. When he got inside of a black van he closed the door and winked.

"What the fuck was that?" he asked Echo.

"You didn't think I would let Mariah live with you unprotected? Did you?" she laughed. "Listen, you a joke. So do me a favor and lose my fucking number." She hung up, walked back into the bedroom and slipped under the sheets.

"Who was that?" Sapphire asked, snuggling her naked body against Echo's—her warm breasts against her side.

"A nothing ass nigga." She kissed her on the forehead. "Go back to sleep. I'm trying to fuck again in the A.M."

They stood in Nasir's kitchen as classical music played softly in the background.

"I don't care what I said, people change their minds all the time," Sapphire pleaded as she stood behind Nasir as he prepared sushi from scratch, a skill he learned from one of his ex-girlfriends.

"Like I told you the last ten times, it's too late," he said strongly. "I already sent word."

Sapphire felt as if she'd been gut punched. "But things are going smoothly now. And I thought that was why you did all of this in the beginning. For me to be happy." She paused. "We're family, Nasir." Tears rolled down her cheek. "First cousins at that...please don't hurt someone I love."

"I really wish I could. Like you said, we're family, but once things are set in motion you can't stop the roll."

"I don't understand!" she yelled bringing her fist down on the counter. "You have a wife now." She stood in front of him. Looking him in the eyes she asked, "Doesn't she make you happy? Mariah?"

Nasir looked up at her, wiped his hand on the white towel on his shoulder and pushed her to the side. Focusing on packing the rice for the rolls again he said, "Did you slash my tires? Out of jealousy at the club that night? I can see you doing something so foul."

Her face reddened. "No...I...uh..."

"You have to learn to let people go," he said skipping the subject and faking like he wasn't equally crazy. "She has twisted your mind so much that you have no loyalty, not even to me." There was something behind his eyes that she didn't like.

"When I came to you the other week, and said I wanted her taken care of it was because I thought she didn't love me. And that she never would. Now she asked me to be with her, Nasir." She squinted. "But I know now that you never did this for me so it wouldn't have mattered anyway...right?" she paused. "You fell in love with her too. Didn't you?"

"You believe what you want," he said placing his packed sushi roll into the refrigerator. He wiped his hand on his towel again. "I'm not gonna try and change your mind about it."

"I can tell by looking in your eyes that it was never about me."

He moved about the kitchen with a slight grin on his face, as if her troubles were irrelevant. Seeing a knife on the counter she placed the tip of the blade against the bottom of his chin. "Get on the phone and call off your hit man." She yelled. "Do it now before I gut you."

He looked square in her eyes. "Do you know it's hard for me to allow a female to touch my dick sometimes? Every time Mariah tries I jump because I'm afraid she'll cut it off like Echo tried to. That bitch ruined my life and for the first time she'll pay."

She placed the knife on the counter, walked away and leaned against the refrigerator. "You could've got back at her anytime. Why now?"

"There's no statute of limitations on revenge for attempted castration, primo." He placed his hand on her shoulder and looked down at her. "Besides, nothing is as bad as it seems. You'll see...trust me."

Echo and Six sat on the rooftop of a famous restaurant in Washington DC, overlooking the city at night. Since Six was dom and Echo was fem they looked more like a couple than best friends.

"Don't care what you say...you can't eat no pussy like that," Echo laughed right before pulling on the hookah lamp pipe. The cherry flavor smoke filled her lungs before she released it into the city. "Not without her ass sitting on your face anyway."

Six chuckled. "On everything I love, the bitch was on all fours and I was eating it just like that. All you gotta do is lift them cheeks and get at it that way." She paused. "Let me show you." She winked and moved toward her.

Echo slapped her hand. "I ain't fucking with you."

"I know you ain't gonna give me none of that pussy because you scared I would have your ass geeking." She smiled. "But what you should do is hook me up with Kari's sexy self."

"She's straight and off limits. Leave it alone."

"Not until I get at her," Six laughed.

"Your lips gonna fall off from all the pussy you be eating."

"Nigga, you get way more than I do." She laughed wiping her mouth. "Don't get mad because you just like me. Too freaked out."

"That might be true but you talking crazy now." Echo looked out at the city and sighed.

Six noticed her sudden mood change. "Uh, oh. What's on your mind?"

"Ever made a mistake and want to take it back but don't have a good enough reason?" she gazed at her friend and back at the city.

Six's eyebrows lowered. "What you mean?"

"I told Sapphire we would be together. Moved her in my spot and everything. But something don't feel right...yet nothing else out here for me."

"Why would you do that shit, son?" Six said falling back into her seat. "We haven't even met this chick yet."

"I know...I know. On the surface shit looks legit. She has a little boutique out Philly and drives out there a lot through the week, which is why you never see her. For real that's the only reason I can tolerate her, she not always up under me."

"Do you love her?"

"Ain't you listening, nigga? Not even close." She paused. "But I'm tired of being alone too. Tired of sleeping with a new bitch every night with no commitment. I'm ready to settle down."

"But with a stranger?"

"It's in the cards I guess." She shrugged.

"You doing this because Mariah's taken?"

"Nah...she moved on and I did too," she said confidently.

Six nodded and took the hookah pipe, not believing shit she was popping. "I heard you rapping 'bout this Mariah chick for months in lock up. She was all you could talk about. And now you home and you act like it wasn't real. Ain't she worth fighting for, Echo?" She pulled on the pipe and released smoke. "Don't let her get away because her situation with dude *looks* permanent. You Echo Kelly...you always get the bitch. Why should now be any different?"

Faith sat in the back of Echo's limo looking a hot ass mess...

Her hair was matted and hadn't been combed in weeks and although she tried to hide it by stuffing it in a yellow headscarf, Echo could still see it was unkempt.

"The nigga Donte is not who you think he is, Faith," Echo pleaded as she stared at her friend. "You should've stayed with Barry. He may not be the nigga you wanted but he would kill for you."

"You don't even know him," Faith yelled. "He cares about me and I care about him. I mean I chose another dude...I don't understand why it's such a big deal with you and my sister."

"Faith, the nigga Donte does this kind of shit all the time. He finds women who are on the come up or got a lot going for themselves. Then he sees how many of them he can get strung out on drugs. When he gets them hooked on crack he places their pictures on a website and under it marks how long it took. It's a game to him." She reached in her purse and pulled out a piece of paper. She handed it to her. "This is you and he has under your name four months."

Faith snatched it from her hand and scanned it. She noticed the other girls on the sheet too and felt gut punched after seeing one of them was her friend. Handing it back she said, "How I know he did this?"

"Fuck!" Echo yelled. "Because I wouldn't lie to you! Why you not listening? You want me to kill this mothafucka? Huh? Because that's what I'll do if you keep dealing with him!"

"No!" Faith said with wide eyes. "I want you to stay away from him, Echo. This is my business."

"But you my friend."

Faith exhaled. "I know...but I'm not brown skin or pretty like you," she said with tears rolling down her face. "Girls as dark as me don't have a lot of options these days. We gotta go with the dude who wants us the most."

Echo raised her eyebrows. "And you think that's Donte instead of Barry?"

"Echo, please..."

"First off there's nothing wrong with your complexion. Is that what the nigga wants you to believe? Because it ain't true.," she asked passionately. "Faith, you're beautiful. You could have any man you want, but if you don't take care of yourself you'll never believe me. Don't buy into that dark skin light skin bullshit because I know plenty of darker women who run rings around lighter ones. It's all about confidence."

"I didn't do it you know?" Faith said skipping the subject. "I didn't kill Aspen but half of my life was spent behind bars. I'm home now...and all I want is someone to love me back." She paused and wiped a tear from her face. "Do you believe me? That I didn't kill her?"

"Yes...you know I do."

Faith exhaled. "Are you still gonna tell the cops? About me stealing your purse?"

"No...just said that shit so you would get back in contact with me."

Faith smiled. "I'm sorry I stole your shit, and I appreciate you not snitching but you gotta let me live my life."

Echo had thoughts of stepping to Donte anyway. "I don't know if I can do that...get out of the way I mean." She paused. "This nigga is single handedly taking my friend down to the gutter."

Faith looked down at her grungy hands and back at her. "I'm begging you. Don't get into my business because you would hate for somebody to get into yours." She paused. "Promise me, Echo. Promise me now."

Echo's right leg shook rapidly. Slowly she turned her head and glanced out the window at her bodyguards. "You got that. You won't have no problems with me."

"Good," she smiled. "Can I have some money?"

"I'ma be one hundred. As long as you doing this drug shit, I don't have nothing for you, Faith."

Her brows lowered. "Fine...but if somebody kills me because I'm trying to make a couple of dollars it's your fault." She exited the car and dipped down the block.

Echo threw her head back and exhaled.

When she left Arnold slid into the car. "Want me to have my men watch her?"

"No," she sighed. "But if the nigga Donte gets hit by a car I won't be mad."

He smiled. "Let me see if I can make it happen."

CHAPTER FIFTEEN
GAYS GOT A CHOICE TOO

Taja sat in the passenger seat of Kari's new ride, listening to music. "It doesn't bother me anymore. I'm over that shit."

"Yeah right," Kari said as she steered the car.

"For real," Taja said as she dug through her purse. "It's her life not mine."

"How come I don't believe you?"

"You don't have to believe me, bitch." She shrugged. "And I'm not surprised." She removed a pack of cigarettes from her purse. The habit fell in her lap recently after arguing with her long time boyfriend Glo, who wouldn't commit to marriage. "People hardly believe anything I say anyway."

Kari looked over at Taja and laughed. "That's good because with Echo moving in with her girlfriend not a lot is changing."

"You met her?"

"A few times in passing. It's like she makes up excuses not to be around Echo's friends."

"Maybe she knows we'd be on to her shit." Taja looked out of the window, lit her cigarette and inhaled. "I just wish mama would stop giving Echo such a hard time though."

"Echo tried reaching out again?"

"Tried to reach out is an understatement. She's sent my mother cards, letters, flowers...but nothing works. As long as she's gay she's pretty much dead to hear my mother tell it."

Kari sighed. "That's an awful thing to do...to live with hate on your heart for so long. For your own child. Nobody in they right mind wants to be gay anyway."

"Who told you that shit?" Taja asked with wide eyes.

"It's the truth. As much shit as gays go through...who would want to live that lifestyle? Unless you're born that way I don't see too many people signing up."

"My sister for starters," she laughed. "She was gay before it was fashionable but I know she could've went the other way if she wanted. Plenty of boys liked her but she gave them the blues."

"You contradicting yourself. Saying the same thing I am. If it ain't got a pussy you can best be certain that Echo not fucking with it. She's your sister but I know her way better than you." Kari shook her head and saw she had a text message from Faith. When she reached the light she read it.

Faith: My man dead.

"What the fuck?" Kari said to herself. She tried calling Faith as she continued to drive but she wasn't answering.

"What happened?" Taja asked in a concern tone.

"Faith just said her man dead"

"Donte or Barry?"

"Not sure." She placed her phone back in the console.

"I'm not surprised the nigga dead, she probably did that shit," Taja said rolling her eyes.

"Fuck you say some shit like that to me for?" she paused. "You acting like my sister serial with her shit. She killed one person...and if I know her it was out of self defense."

"All I'm saying is that Faith has the potential." She paused. "Shit...I do too for that matter."

"You could kill someone?"

"In a heartbeat."

Kari pulled up behind Benita's car in front of her new house in Upper Marlboro, Maryland.

Taja took another pull and tossed the cigarette out the window. "I'll be back."

"Aye, Taja, don't be in there running your mouth with your mother all night. That's why I'm not going in because time is not on my side. Just get your mail and bring your killer ass back out. I got a lot of shit to do today."

"I got you, bitch. Relax."

"Fuck that. I'm doing you a favor cause your car in the shop but I know how your slow ass is! Speed it up."

"You doing the most," Taja rolling her eyes. "It ain't like I don't do shit for you so chill the fuck out."

"Hurry up."

Taja eased out of the car and walked toward her mother's house.

Bored out of her mind Kari texted Echo.

Kari: I think Barry dead.
Echo: WTF?!
Kari: No details yet. But what's the word?
Echo: With?

Kari smiled.

Kari: Mariah.
Echo: Nothing. We just friends.
Kari: Seeing her anytime soon?
Echo: U trying 2 get Sapphire 2 kill me?
Kari: Haven't met the bitch but I can tell I don't like her already. She standing in the way of true love.
Echo: lol. Don't worry. U don't have to like her or fuck her. I do.

Kari was still smiling when she heard Taja screaming inside the house. Horrified she dropped her phone in the passenger seat and took off running toward the house. When she opened the door and saw Taja's light skin flushed red, and blood on her shirt, she walked closer.

Within seconds she saw Benita stretched out on the floor with a bullet wound to her head.

Echo and Sapphire were walking arm and arm in Washington DC, with several large Hermes bags in their hands. As usual bodyguards followed, always checking the surroundings, making it easier for Echo to be at ease.

Despite the protection Sapphire on the other hand looked uncomfortable. Often looking behind herself as if she were being chased.

When Echo's phone dinged she saw she had a text message. Removing it from her pocket she read the details.

Mariah: Get the ID yet?
Echo: No...but I'll hit U when I do.

When she was done she looked at Sapphire who had an attitude.

"What's been on your mind?" Echo asked.

Sapphire removed her arm, crossed her arms over her chest and looked at her as they continued to walk. "Nothing. I was just thinking about my shop that's all."

"You lying now?" she paused. "Because that's a fucked up way to start a relationship."

"I'm not lying I just...I guess I know who you are. So sometimes it's hard for me to be as laid back as you."

Echo frowned. "Meaning?"

"You a drug dealer, Echo. And dealers are revered and hated. That means somebody can come for me at any moment. You gotta excuse me if I'm not so comfortable walking down the street."

"But you with me. And if you with me that means I won't let anyone hurt you. I don't care who it is."

"I know." She smiled.

Suddenly Six's truck pulled up alongside the curb and parked sideways in a rushed manner.

Echo and Sapphire jumped back.

Although the bodyguards knew her, they didn't allow her in Echo's path when she hopped out of the truck due to her anxiousness. It didn't stop Six from trying to bogart her way through.

Knowing her best friend would never hurt her she said, "It's fine," Six moved closer. "What's up?"

Six's energy was excitable in a negative way. "I been trying to reach you!" she yelled out of breath. "Where's your phone?"

"Don't worry 'bout that. You got me now. So what's up?"

"It's your mother...your mother." Six couldn't complete the sentence.

"Just say it!"

"It's your mother...she's gone."

While Echo was inside of her mother's house trying to console Taja, and dodge questions from police, Sapphire was outside on the phone.

Because Six's truck was oversized she used it to hide behind as she held a serious phone conversation. "Why would you do that shit?" she asked angrily.

"I told you it was too late," Nasir said calmly. "You thought it was a game."

"But her mother? Who goes after innocent people?"

"Who gives a fuck about that bitch...she ain't my mother?"

Sapphire looked toward the left, and at the house, to be sure no one was coming. When the coast was clear she said, "What if I tell her you did it? Then what you gonna do?"

"Tell who what?" Six asked walking up behind Sapphire, scaring her half to death. Six's stare was intense as she waited for an answer. "And why you tucked behind my truck while your girl is inside?"

"Uh...I...too much was going on and I wanted to hang out here. Trying to stay out the way." Sapphire hung up the phone and stuffed it in her pocket. "I was talking to a friend...we were...I mean..."

"What you talking to a friend about out here?" Six grilled. "And why you refuse to come in the house?"

"Something private."

"I got my eyes on you, bitch." Six pointed in her face. "And when Echo gets through what she's going through I'm going to tell her I don't trust your ass."

Sapphire dropped the sweet routine. "Don't fuck with me, Six, or whatever they call you." She stepped closer. "You don't know what I'm capable of."

Six wasn't the least bit afraid. "We'll see about that." She paused. "Won't we?"

CHAPTER SIXTEEN
SWEET ACCUSATIONS

Echo's mansion was bustling with people who attended the funeral earlier and wanted to offer condolences, a bit longer than she desired.

In the dining room, away from the crowd, sat Echo, Six, Kari, Faith and Sapphire. Taja was there earlier but the pain of losing her mother was too great and she needed to be alone— away from the crowd.

Sapphire, who hadn't said one word to Echo's friends, rubbed Echo's shoulders. "Can I get you anything, baby? Something hard to drink?"

"I just need some air that's all." Which was code word for *leave me the fuck alone.*

Instead of bouncing, Sapphire looked down at Echo's black Christian Louboutin pumps, dropped to her knees and removed her shoes. Everybody in the room stared at her like she was crazy, especially when she started massaging her feet.

"Aye, Sapphire...just leave me alone," Echo said firmly. "I just need five minutes...please."

Sapphire stood up and dusted off her knees. "Okay, I'll bring some more ice water." Sapphire removed a silver pitcher off the table and walked toward the kitchen. She wasn't at the funeral earlier but did her best to make sure Echo was comfortable afterwards. After all, it was partially her fault.

When she was gone Echo waved Arnold over. When he came she said, "Get everybody out my house. Everybody but whoever is in this room."

"Sure thing," he said going to handle business.

When he was gone Six walked up to Echo and said, "I know this the wrong time but I really got to talk to you 'bout something. If I thought it could wait I would."

"If it's more bad news then leave it alone," Echo responded, eyes red as blood. "I can only deal with but so much today."

"I understand that...I do...it's just that it may not be able to wait. I'm afraid if I don't say something now then something worse will happen later."

Echo wiped her eyes and looked up at her. "What you saying?"

"I don't trust your girlfriend. I have a feeling she was involved with what happened to your mother."

"Hold up, Six," Kari said with her hand extended. "You making huge accusations now."

"Which is why I don't take what I'm saying lightly."

"How you figure she was involved?" Echo frowned.

"I walked behind her and overheard her talking to somebody on the phone the day your mother was discovered. And it ain't sound good. She was all tucked behind my truck and shit whispering. Like she was hiding."

"What was said?" Echo continued.

"Something about she should tell her what you did." She paused. "I get the impression she was telling whoever was on the phone that she was going to let you in on the murder."

"So basically you not sure." Echo said through squinted eyes. "Is that what you're telling me?

Accusing somebody of killing my mother is heavy."

"I know it sound bad, Echo," Six admitted. "This is why it took me so long to come to you. But I can't hold back no more. That chick give me bad vibes."

"I don't know what Six is talking about but I've been feeling the same way, Echo," Kari said under her breath. "I've seen her a few times standing in the corner when we're talking. It's like she doesn't want to be around but still wants to know what we're doing. Like she's keeping tabs on us and shit."

Echo's temples throbbed and she rubbed them. "She's my girlfriend. If you want me to feel I can't trust her you have to give me something more. Because right now ya'll making a bad situation worse."

"You know I want you happy," Six said compassionately. "We all do." She paused. "But maybe she's not the one."

"No, maybe you not the one," Echo snapped.

"What?" Six said.

"Tell the truth. You don't want me to be in a relationship," Echo continued standing up. "You like being my little sidekick while you fuck a new bitch every week on my dime. Well I'm tired of living like that. I'm done."

"Fuck is you talking 'bout, Echo?" she yelled. "That girl got you so tied up you can't see your friend is coming at you on some real shit?"

"What I see is that today I buried my mother. And instead of you being here to support you're trying to tear me down."

Having had enough, Faith walked out of the dining room and toward the back door.

"I'm going to check on my sister," Kari said, leaving also.

"Why don't you do me a favor and bounce too, Six," Echo said. "Today is only for friends and family. And it's obvious you're not either."

"You going to regret coming at me like this," Six said. "I promise you that."

"Maybe..." she shrugged. "But not today."

When Six left Sapphire walked back out with a pitcher full of ice water with strawberries inside, as if on queue. Looking around she said, "What happen? Where's everybody?"

"You tell me," Echo said sharply. The roots were planted in her mind about Sapphire and it caused the trust to falter even more.

"I don't know what you mean?" Sapphire sat in a chair next to her. "What's going on, baby?"

"Are you doing right by me? Can I really trust you?"

With a smile she said, "Echo, you know that—"

"I need you to answer the fucking question straight up. Can I trust you or not?"

"Yes...of course you can."

"Then why Six making me feel that I made a mistake by choosing you?" she frowned. "Huh? What happened at my mother's house?"

Sapphire moved around uneasily in her seat. "I didn't want to tell you this but you leaving me no choice. The other day, the day you found your mother, she tried to hit on me while I was by her truck."

"Fuck you talking 'bout?"

"I know it sounds crazy but it's true." She touched her hand. "And when I told her I was with you she got mad."

Echo pulled away. "I don't know what shit you on but I know my friend. The last thing she would do is disrespect. Especially on the day I lost my mother."

"It's true," Sapphire pleaded. "I have no reason to lie."

"I'm going upstairs. And don't come up tonight. I want to be left alone.

Echo sat on the edge of her bed with her cell phone in one hand and a sheet of paper with just a number in the other. When she was ready she dialed the digits for someone she only knew as Goon. Looking out into her room, her left leg shook rapidly as she waited. It only rang twice before it was answered. Hesitantly she said, "You don't know me...but my name's Echo."

"I was told you would call," the voice said. "Was given this number and told to expect you."

Echo was slightly relieved that at least the Goon was familiar. "I need your services."

"The full treatment or location?"

"For now the location. And I need...I need...to know if my girl was involved."

Echo felt slight betrayal for even thinking the idea but she needed to be sure. Her heart told her it was Nasir, but the person who killed Benita was allowed into her home. Although Benita knew him Echo doubted they would be keeping time with one another. She would've killed him and thought about it later but Mariah's apparent love for him had her stunted.

At the end of the day she needed to be sure.

"Give me as much information as possible. And I'll see what I can do."

Kari sat next to her sister on the steps leading to Echo's yard, and rubbed her back softly. Faith was an emotional wreck Kari felt it had more to do with her drug habit than Benita dying.

"Remember when we were kids and would run away from home?" Faith paused. "I'm talking 'bout before Aunt Kim came to get us and we lived with her."

"Yep...ma would trick us to come back by yelling out the window how much she loved us to the neighborhood and shit. And that if anybody saw us they should tell us to come back."

"We fell for it every time," Faith continued wiping her nose. "All she wanted was them checks Aunt Kim use to drop on her ass. It was never about us."

Kari gazed down at her torn up sister. She looked nothing like she did when Echo cleaned her up; during the first few days she was free from prison. "Sis, I want to ask something but please don't be mad...are you using drugs? Are you doing what mama did?"

Silence.

"Faith, are you on drugs?" Kari asked firmer.

"I didn't do it," Faith said softly. She looked back at her and then out at the yard again. "I didn't kill Aspen."

"What are you talking about? You admitted to it. I heard you myself."

"I admitted to it because ma was about to try and get us back from Aunt Kim, and I didn't want to live with her." She wiped her face again. "Figured it would be better to stay in jail than to move back in that nasty ass apartment. At least I would have a meal everyday and some place safe to sleep."

"If that's the truth why didn't you tell me?" she paused. "I could've fought for you."

"You couldn't do nothing." She waved her off. "Plus I told my lawyer before the trial because I got scared. He said if I tried to change my plea things would be worse. I could get more time and all I wanted to do was my bid and come home. So I never said anything to you."

"Oh my god, Faith," Kari said hugging her tightly. "Did you tell anyone?"

"Later I told Aunt Kim, but she was too heartbroken to hear what I was saying. I think our relationship is fucked up to this day because of that shit."

"She loves you...just wants the best for us that's all."

"Well how come she doesn't answer the phone for me?"

Kari didn't have an answer.

"Exactly," Faith continued. "She fucks with you but not me. That's the story of my life though. Always the shit end of the stick."

Kari looked out at Echo's vast backyard. "I think you remind her of her sister...of mama.

Every time you call you want money and that shit hurts."

"That's not it."

"It's true," Kari continued. "But is she the only one you told about Aspen?"

"And Echo...but you know what, I don't think she ever believed I did it. I think she knew it wasn't me the whole time."

Kari leaned back slightly. "What you saying?"

Faith looked dead in her eyes. "You know what I'm saying."

"So you think Echo murdered Aspen?"

Silence.

"Faith, that's a heavy statement and you shouldn't go around saying it without facts." She paused. "Does it have anything to do with Echo cutting you off financially?"

"It ain't about that," she paused. "I was the only one in prison whose commissary reached the maximum contribution every month. I think she kept me stocked up because she felt guilty for me doing time for a crime she committed."

"I don't believe she has it in her to kill anyone," Kari said straight up.

"But you believe I do?" she paused. "It figures." She shook her head.

"You were always so angry...even when we were coming up...I just..."

"You asked me if I was using drugs a minute ago. I didn't answer because I'm ashamed. Plus who goes into prison drug free but comes out with a habit? Who does that kind of shit? But my mind was so fucked up I needed a release."

"I'm sorry, Faith."

"Poor little Faith," she said. "Everyone feels sorry for me. Well, I'm not a pet. And I will never be." She paused. "But I guess I'm not totally innocent either."

She frowned. "What you mean?"

"I didn't kill Aspen but I took out Donte's fake ass," she said with a sly smile. "It was the best thing I could've done. The look on his face when I brought that knife through his chest...past the bone...past the cartilage." She giggled. "You can't pay for those kinds of moments. Gotta be up close to put the work in yourself, know what I'm saying."

Kari scooted back a little. "Faith...what are you talking about?"

"Found out he wasn't the man I thought he was. Was just using me in a game, so I used him back." She sighed. "Don't worry, if I didn't do it Echo would have. I know it."

"So you're a killer now?" Kari's heart rate was so fast she was on the verge of hyperventilating.

"Why look so surprised, big sis?" Faith smirked. "You believe that about me anyway." She walked back into the house leaving Kari to her thoughts.

In his own house, Keith held Nasir by the throat, his body trembling as he wrestled with taking his own son's life. When he realized his wife would never forgive him, or he himself, he allowed him to fall to the floor.

"Get up," Keith said breathing heavily.

Nasir used the wall to pull himself up, his legs felt like spaghetti under his body.

"I told you not to mess with her." He pointed at him. "I told you it would bring us trouble and you did it anyway. All of your life you failed to listen and now your incompetence has affected me! Has affected this family!"

Nasir rubbed his throbbing throat and hacked a few times to catch his breath. "I didn't bother her, dad. It was—"

"You killed her mother!" he roared, his hands clenching into fists. "You never involve an enemy's mother, Nasir...especially while yours is still alive. What were you thinking? Are you that blind that you can't see the trouble you've caused?"

"I'm sorry, dad..."

"You have no idea the amount of misfortune you have brought on this family. She contacted a professional hitter— Goon. It's just a matter of time. I hope you're happy."

"The...*The Goon*?" he stuttered having been familiar with the moniker. It was evident by his wide eye stare that he finally realized he'd gone too far.

"I told you to leave it alone, Nasir. Now you'll see what it means to be in the big leagues. Now you'll see what it's like to be hunted." He paused. "Get out of my house. I have a lot of preventive measures to take."

CHAPTER SEVENTEEN
DIPPED IN CRAZY

Sapphire stood in the middle of the kitchen after having prepared a homemade chicken soup for Echo, who was out in the field getting her soldiers in order. Only a week since the funeral and already her men were slacking.

Echo's troubles may have pertained to losing her mother and money, but Sapphire had problems of her own too. Ever since Echo came to her about Six she had been distant and Sapphire needed to do all she could to win her back.

She'd come so far to gaining her love.

It was time to go harder.

She just finished preparing a fresh salad to go along with the soup when she heard the front door open. A wide smile covered her face as she wiped her hand on the strawberry apron and walked toward the living room, in anticipation of seeing Echo. But she felt like shitting on herself when she saw the last person on earth she wanted to see, the one she'd been avoiding... *Taja.*

"Harper, what are you doing here?" Taja asked placing her purse on the sofa. Her gaze was murderous as she waited for Sapphire's answer.

Sapphire did her best to pretend she wasn't Harper but her horrified facial expression said otherwise. "You must be mistaken. I never met you."

"Is that why you didn't ask me who I was? Because you don't know me?" she laughed. "Stop with the games. We were friends for over half my life. Since daycare. I might not have seen you in over ten years but I know Harper when I see her, no matter how much plastic surgery you've obviously undergone."

Sapphire walked toward the kitchen and Taja followed. "Like I said, you must have me mistaken."

As if Taja remembered something she said, "Wait, are you Echo's new girlfriend?" Her frown was intense.

"I am, but all this other shit you talking about me being someone else is ridiculous." She removed the pot from the stove and stirred briskly. "Who are you exactly?" she continued attempting to cover her tracks. "One of Echo's friends?"

"Bitch, you know me!" Taja observed her new face and body, courtesy of a top rate plastic surgeon and shook her head. "But this new look explains why Echo has no idea who you are and I can't wait to tell her."

Tiring of lying Sapphire removed the spoon from the pot, cut the eye off and walked over toward her. "I love Echo." She placed the spoon on the counter. "And the past is the past and I ask that you keep it that way."

"The past ain't the past unless all members are informed. Because as much shit as you put her through—"

"*We* put her through," Sapphire corrected. "I wasn't the only one chasing her around DC. As I recall you were right there with me, taunting her for being gay." She walked over to the counter and leaned against it. "What do you want? Money? Because I'll do what I have to, to keep this private."

"My sister takes care of me. I'm good on dough but thanks, boo."

"Then what is it, Taja?"

She shook her head. "Either you tell her or I will."

"No you won't," Sapphire laughed. "You and I both know it."

"How you figure?"

"Because my secret isn't the only one being kept from Echo."

Taja's face reddened. "That was an accident."

"It doesn't matter because at the end of the day you killed *my* sister. So if we gonna tell a story let's tell it all."

Frazzled, Taja walked into the living room and this time Sapphire followed. She plopped down on the sofa and threw her hands in her face. "It wasn't like that."

"I know...I was a real friend and despite losing my twin I kept your secret. All I'm asking is that you do the same for me. Why hurt Echo more than she has been already?"

"I mean what is all this?" Taja asked crying uncontrollably. "Why are you posted up around my sister? Why you lying?"

Silence.

"Wait...you were always obsessed with her." Taja continued wiping her tears. "Weren't you?"

"Not obsession. Love." She paused. "And if you try to make the situation any other way I will alert the police about Aspen, I swear to God. Is that what you want?"

"I said it was an accident! She wouldn't leave me alone when I didn't feel like being bothered. So I...So I..."

"So you pushed her," Sapphire said with a crazy smile on her face. "Down a flight of concrete steps to her death."

"She wasn't dead!" Taja yelled jumping up. "I wanted to call the ambulance. I even begged but you the one who didn't want to."

"But for the push I wouldn't have needed to call for help. So it still makes it your fault."

"You watched your own sister die. And then you...then you..."

"Did what needed to be done to make it look right. To make it believable."

"No!" She pointed in her face. "You didn't need to remove her clothes and ram her with a branch in her vagina...while she was still alive!"

"It had to look like a rape. It was the only way to keep Echo safe. Don't play naive, Taja. Had we not done that your sister would've been in prison longer than that little stint she did. Remember? Aspen and me fought her that day after school. And what better way to get revenge then murder? Of course they would've believed it was her."

Taja felt exhausted with it all. "How long have you been trying to get at Echo? How long have you been playing this game?"

"If you must know since high school. I'm the one who had my cousin Nasir try to come onto Echo. I wanted her away from Mariah, but I guess she was really into girls because she never bit. All it did was make me want her more. And then that stupid mothafuckin cousin of mine fell in love."

Taja stood up again. "Nasir is your cousin?"

Silence.

"If you liked her why did you put her through so much shit?"

"Because she didn't like me back," she said through squinted eyes.

By T. Styles   177

Taja was seeing red. "I want you out of my sister's house."

"Ain't you listening...I'm not going anywhere."

"Then I'll go to the cops."

"You do that. And my story won't match yours I promise. I'll tell the cops that you killed Aspen and then you'll be locked away. Which won't be a bad idea now that I think about it. This way I'll get to have her all to myself and it won't be a thing you can do about it. Tell me, Taja. Is it worth all the trouble?"

Echo woke up in a better mood than she'd been in weeks. She figured life was going to bring her ups and downs so she had to pick herself up. Rolling over in bed she gazed at Sapphire who was staring into her eyes. There wasn't a day that had gone by when Sapphire wasn't up before Echo...staring at her intently. As if she didn't believe being with her was real.

"Let's do something tonight," Echo said.

Sapphire's eyes widened with excitement. "Sure...What?"

"Let's go to a club."

Sapphire's happy expression wiped away. "I hate clubs, baby. You know that. I prefer solo shit so I can enjoy you alone." The last thing she needed was being recognized by someone else.

"I forgot." Echo lay on her back.

"How 'bout we take a boat ride on the Baltimore Harbor, just you, and me." Sapphire suggested. "You have a yacht that you never use. Commission a captain and let's cruise."

Echo started to shoot the idea down until she gave it a little more consideration. "You know what...that's a good idea."

Taja sat on the edge of a bed in a cheap motel—Six and Kari stared down at her. "Thanks for coming," she told them. "I know it was last minute so I really appreciate it."

When Kari saw a spider crawl up a wall nearest her, she almost screamed. Moving out the way she asked, "Why are we here again? Because this is the nastiest run down place I've ever been in my life."

"I had to pick a spot no one would ever think we'd come," Taja said. "So excuse the accommodations. We won't be here long."

"So what's up?" Six asked, hands stuffed in her pockets.

"I asked you both here because there's a big problem. With Sapphire."

Irritated about the mentioning of her name, Six moved toward the door. "I'll get up with ya'll later."

Kari stood in front of it, blocking her exit. "Don't do this, Six. You here now. The least you can do is hear her out."

"You don't understand. I was a rider for Echo and she did the ultimate. Put a bitch before me. So I'm gonna leave her to it and just hope for the best."

"So this an ego thing?" Taja asked.

"It ain't about an ego, it's about letting a friend make her own bed," Six continued. She twisted the knob and opened the door.

"Let her go, Kari," Taja said. "I thought she was a real friend. I won't make the same mistake again."

Six got so heated her skin reddened. Closing the door she rushed up to Taja and said, "Ain't nobody more loyal to Echo than me."

"Then act like it," Taja responded. "Get out of your feelings because I need your help."

Six walked up to the wall and leaned against it. "Go 'head."

"Sapphire is not who Echo thinks she is," Taja explained. "Her real name is Harper."

Kari's eyes widened. "Get the fuck out of here! Fat Harper from 'round the way? The one we used to fight? Your friend?"

"I know...don't rub it in. I'm embarrassed enough as is."

"But she doesn't look anything like Harper." Kari continued.

"Well she is. The last thing I would do was play with ya'll like this. Despite the new body she ain't nothing but Fat Face Harper from southeast. Just paid for a lot of plastic surgery that's all."

"If it's true, if Echo finds out she would go the fuck off."

"Exactly," Taja said.

"That dirty bitch," Kari responded. "I knew I ain't like her fucking ass!"

"So why don't you just tell her?" Six asked. "And be done with it."

"Because I can't," Taja said under her breath. "Just trust me when I say it has to be done a different way."

"So what's the plan?" Kari asked.

"I figured out a way to make the bitch tell on herself." Taja looked up at both of them. "But I'll need your help."

"What does it involve?" Six asked.

"Since Harper was a kid she had a photosensitivity," Taja explained. "Went to a carnival once and she seized out due to the bright lights. Echo knows this and if we do it right, and Harper has a seizure, Echo may remember and see the resemblance." She paused. "It's all I got but it's worth a try. My only question is are you guys with me?"

Six and Kari looked at one another and nodded their heads. "I'm in if ya'll are," Six responded.

Earlier in the day Kari was excited when she called Echo. She told her to come to a location and bring Sapphire too.

So she did.

When Echo arrived at the dark sexy restaurant in a hotel which overlooked Washington DC, she was shocked to see Six, Kari and Mariah were present. A bottle of expensive champagne sat in a gold ice bucket on the table and she smiled. "Wow, this is a surprise," Echo said as she pulled a seat out for Sapphire who stunned everyone in a beautiful black dress with major cleavage.

Echo was just as sexy— dipped in a designer cat suit that gave every curve on her body it's own shine. There wasn't a man present who didn't imagine how it would be to have both of them at the same time.

She took a seat next to Sapphire.

"We heard the news," Kari said looking at Sapphire's smug face. It took all she had to not call Sapphire out on her bullshit, but things had to be done correctly. Besides, they rehearsed the night repeatedly with Taja and it would be a shame for things to not go down as planned.

"And we wanted to support," Six added.

"All of us..." Mariah said with a smile. She looked more brokenhearted than supportive. "That's what this is about."

She wasn't the only one.

Echo felt uncomfortable sitting across from Mariah while she pledged her heart to another, not knowing she was Harper. The thought was fleeting when she remembered she was married to Nasir. It was time to move on with her life.

"Where is your ring?" Kari asked Sapphire. "I was so excited to see it."

"It was a last minute thing, but the proper diamond is being fitted now," Echo said.

"Seems rushed if you ask me," Mariah admitted. "But as long as you're happy. Or trying to be."

"Rushed or not it still won't stop me from being Mrs. Kelly," she winked.

Mariah rolled her eyes.

"So how does it feel, nigga?" Six said tapping Echo playfully on the shoulder. "Your pretty ass finally 'bout to get hitched."

Echo looked over at Mariah and then away. "Feels good." She moved uncomfortably. "Was starting to think it would never happen for me. Glad it ain't true."

Sapphire played it calm but she didn't fuck with any of Echo's friends. Besides, she knew Kari from back when and didn't like her then. Now isn't any different. And the moment they talked sideways she had intentions of using the gun nestled in her purse.

"So what is tonight about?" Echo asked looking around.

"It's your engagement party," Mariah said. "After we heard from Kari you were getting married we decided to put a little something together. I'm sure you'll have another...but this is just for us."

"How sweet." Sapphire stated. "Seems like ya'll came around suddenly. Too good to be true." She paused. "Was almost getting use to the fact that everybody here would hate me. Surprise, surprise."

"When you love someone as much as we do Echo you do what you have to," Kari added.

Sapphire looked all of them over.

Something didn't feel right.

"Where's Taja?" Echo asked. It had been weeks since she'd spoken to her sister and surprisingly she missed her.

"Couldn't be here," Mariah said. "But she sends her love."

"No more gloom...I propose a toast," Six said removing the champagne from the bucket. Ice slivers dripped to the table as she raised it in the air. She grabbed a gold-rimmed champagne glass and sat one in front of Sapphire. "Let's set this party off right." She loosened the cork and it popped, bringing with it a puff of white foam down the bottle.

"Hold fast, Six," Kari said, stopping her from pouring.

Six lowered her arm and Kari looked behind her. She waved over a group of photographers who sat in the corner, large professional cameras in hand. "We need pictures before we get white girl wasted."

"I don't want to take a picture," Sapphire said seriously. "But you guys are welcome to it."

"Why not?" Echo smiled, in a way better mood since her mother died. "My friends really trying to make this nice, baby. Give them a little help."

"It's just not me that's all," she said standing up, preparing to leave.

"Do it for me," Echo demanded pulling her back down. "Give them a chance."

Sapphire took a seat just as the photographers converged on the table. Before she could even check her makeup they were bombarding her with flashing lights, causing her eyes to throb. It seemed like every photographer was focused on Sapphire, as she was hit with flash after flash.

When it was getting ridiculous Echo stood up, "Hold up...what's going on?" she asked the photographers.

"More pictures!" Kari yelled to them, angry Sapphire hadn't fallen into a seizure. The plan was to bombard her with lights so that she would fall ill but it wasn't working. "She's getting married! And we want her to have the best."

"I said stop!" Echo yelled.

There was one problem. She hadn't paid them so the men ignored her. They were given specific orders, to get up in the woman's face who had the only champagne glass before her. That meant Sapphire.

When none of the photographers would listen to Echo she snapped her fingers and the place was suddenly flooded with her men. She instructed them to stay outside of the restaurant earlier, because she didn't want to ruin the ambiance. Now she needed their help.

"Get them out of here," she ordered as they surrounded the table. "Take them cameras too."

One by one the bodyguards collected the men and their cameras. When the restaurant was quiet again she gazed down at her friends, who looked as guilty as a dog that shitted on the living room floor. "What the fuck was that about?"

"They wanted to humiliate me," Sapphire said before standing up. She knew they were trying to trip her into a seizure but she had since outgrown them. "When are you going to realize, Echo? They don't like me." She ran toward the exit and with a wave Echo directed one of her men to see her to the car safely.

Focusing on her friends she said, "I love her."

"Are you sure?" Mariah asked. "Because a few days ago judging by the way you looked at me, I thought you loved me too."

"You thought wrong," Echo snapped. "And if ya'll can't get with her it means you don't care about me."

"We do care about you," Mariah said. "That's why we're—"

"Jealous!" Echo shot back. "I take care of every one of you in this room but the moment I want a life of my own there's a problem." She stood up, reached in her purse and dropped a thousand dollars on the table. "Don't stop the party on account of me." She walked out.

In the back of the limo, Sapphire leaned against Echo's shoulder and wept. "I told you they hated me," she sobbed. "I can't be around them anymore, Echo! I just can't!"

"I know, baby." She rubbed her shoulder. "From here on out I'll meet them alone. You shouldn't have to be subject to that shit."

Sapphire looked at her and scooted away. "You mean you'll still see them? After everything they did to me tonight?"

"They were being jerks but they're my best friends, Sapphire. I can't cut them off forever. I love them too much for that shit."

"So they more important to you than me? Huh? Is that what you're saying?" her eyes looked wild and deranged and for some reason she looked familiar to Echo in a strange way.

But why?

"Don't do this," she said.

"Do what?" Sapphire screamed.

"Aye, Sapphire, I suggest you lower your voice. Before I forget that your feelings are hurt and smack the shit outta you."

"I'm sorry," she said a little lower. "It's just that I don't see anything wrong with demanding that my fiancé treat me with the respect I've been craving from the beginning of our relationship. Don't you see they want to tear us apart?"

"You can't demand anything from me. That's what you forgetting."

When Echo didn't give her the response she wanted she moved toward the door, pushed it open and slipped out.

Echo sighed. "Go watch her," she instructed one of the two men who were in the limo.

When the cell phone beeped in her purse and she saw the text message from Goon her stomach rumbled.

After having read it, slowly she rolled her head until she was focused on Sapphire, who for extra attention was leaning on one of her guards crying outside of the car.

Anger coursed through her blood.

Now it was time for war.

CHAPTER EIGHTEEN
TWO WEEKS LATER
DIAMOND READY

At 1:00pm in the afternoon Echo slinked into the house exhausted before plopping down on the sofa. Over the past few days, things had been stressful and Sapphire did all she could to make her comfortable, attending to her every need, sexually and mentally.

Trying to grab a quick nap, she closed her eyes for a second and when she reopened them Sapphire was standing in front of her wearing a long black trench coat. When she possessed Echo's attention she dropped it to the floor and stood before her, wearing nothing but a sexy red two-piece corset set, a black top hat and a pair of red stilettos with spiked heels.

In that moment she proved why she gained Echo's attention.

Simply put the bitch was bad.

"Hello, sexy," Sapphire said seductively. She grabbed a chair and sat in it backwards. "How was your day?" she opened her legs wide.

Echo smiled, reached into her pocket and removed a small velvet box. "I don't know...how 'bout you tell me."

When Sapphire saw the diamond ring she hopped up from the chair, knocking it over in the process. The sex kitten routine she was about to perform went out the window quickly when she realized she was about to be a wife. To be honest after the restaurant situation some weeks back, she thought Echo may have changed her mind.

Now she discovered that she was wrong.

Overjoyed she dropped to her knees and eased between Echo's legs. Looking up to her she said, "Oh my, god! You didn't!"

Echo removed the ring and slid it on Sapphire's ring finger. "I did...and now it's official." She paused. "I meant what I said, sweetheart. I want you to get everything you deserve."

When the ring was on and it spun around the smile transitioned into a frown. "It doesn't fit," Sapphire pouted. "I've waited all my life for this and it doesn't fit!" Just that quickly her crazy came shining through.

"Don't worry, sweetheart," Echo said softly, calming her down. She placed both hands on her shoulders. "I'll have my driver take you in the limo to get it fitted. To the place I bought it."

"Now?" she asked with wide eyes.

"Can you think of a better time to sport the ring that says you're about to be my wife?"

Sapphire jumped up like the floor was hot. "You're right! I'm gonna get dressed now!"

Sapphire stomped toward the counter at *The Mountebank Diamond* to get with the sales associate about her ring being too loose. Echo assured her she requested the right size, so why didn't it fit?

Armed with the gift receipt she approached the counter with vigilance, her long legs reaching forward as she made her way. When she arrived, a young Latino couple was being helped and she pushed them to the side as if they were irrelevant.

Her rudeness was gross.

The salesman, a large black man with a stare that could kill waited patiently to put her in Sapphire place.

Slamming the receipt on the counter she said, "My fiancé bought me this ring after proposing. And guess what, I can't wear it because it doesn't fit. I'm gonna need you to correct this like a.s.a.p."

"We were here first," the male said.

Sapphire pressed her fingers against his lips to silence him and his woman slapped it away. "Be careful who you touch, bitch. Somebody might take that hand off."

"Come on, honey," the male said pulling her back. "Don't get up with her. I don't even know who would even marry a woman like her."

"No one," the salesman said plainly, folding his arms over his chest. "Not one single person on this planet has intentions on marrying her."

Sapphire focused her efforts on him. With a wide smile on her face she said, "That shows how much you know." She slid the receipt closer and removed the ring from her coat pocket, also placing it on the counter. "For your information I am spoken for. Now fix my shit."

He opened the box and glanced down at the gift receipt, which didn't include a price. "I know who you are," he said flatly. "Sadly enough you don't remember me."

"Should I?" she said rudely.

"You talked about my complexion every day for most of my life in high school. You may have a new body but your attitude is still the same. Now I own this place and I get to see the look on your face when I bust your bubble, courtesy of my girl Echo." He paused. "The name's Monte."

Sapphire still didn't recall nor did she care. "Well if you really know me you should know I don't like my time wasted. Now go see about my ring before I really go off in this bitch."

"I have something for you," he said as the couple looked on with great interest.

He walked away. And when he returned he held a medium sized wood basket filled with Sapphire's favorite treats as a child. There were boxes of *Mike and Ike's*, *Goobers*, and microwave popcorn. Placing it on the table he said, "This is for you, it's worth more than your ring." His smile told her he was in on a joke she wasn't privy to.

Sapphire's face turned flush red. "What is this?"

"You don't remember, Fatty? You may be starving yourself now but this is the shit you ate as a kid." He winked. "It's from your lover. I'm sorry...your ex-fiancé." He reached in the basket and removed a small red envelope. "She even gave you a card, how sweet."

Without reading it she snatched it from his hand. Suddenly everything made sense, to Echo the marriage was all a joke. Sapphire figured Taja put Echo onto who she really was and although she would cry her eyes out later, for now she would try and save face. "Since she wants to play games I want to return this shit. For the money."

"Sure," he shrugged, "but it's not worth what you think."

"Excuse me?" she said through clenched teeth.

"It's fake. A good fake but it never will be a diamond." He smiled wider. "We specialize in look a likes for girls like you who aren't worth it. On the street you won't get more than the fifty bucks Echo paid for it. Now do you really want the money?"

Sapphire felt faint.

Leaving the ring in his possession, she rushed outside to catch some air. Expecting to get in the Porsche limo she felt gut punched when she realized it was gone. At that moment she swore she could feel the earth rotating as she leaned up against the cool brick wall.

Hoping for an answer, she opened the envelope and removed the small card.

It was written in blood.

But whose?

Hello Fat Face Harper. By now you should know that your minutes on earth are numbered. Enjoy every second.

Love E.

Nasir popped up in bed and stared out into the darkness— his breaths heavy and his body dripping wet with sweat. The last thing he remembered was eating dinner with Mariah at a steakhouse before she dropped him off after he complained about being extremely tired. And now, eight hours later he realized he was drugged and she was the culprit.

As he gazed out into the dark room he noticed something was off...way off. Instead of going to search for Mariah he grabbed the remote off the nightstand and turned on the TV, giving the room a little light. But when he saw his mother sitting on a wooden chair with ropes tied around her body on the screen, and a white sock stuffed into her mouth, his heart dropped.

What was happening?

Scooting toward the edge of the bed he hit the play button. His mother's whimpering was loud enough for him to know that he wasn't dreaming.

He immediately began to hyperventilate.

Seconds later Echo appeared behind her, wearing a pair of tight blue jeans and a tight plain t-shirt. He watched her clothing dampen with blood as she brought the knife across her throat...slowly.

"An eye for an eye," Echo said staring into the camera.

Nasir pissed himself.

His father warned him about Echo and that she was no longer the little girl he'd known in high school. Everything about her was different and because of it the family was forced to find out the hard way.

Unable to grieve for his mother and afraid for his own life, he grabbed his car keys off the dresser and slipped into his sneakers. It was time to leave town.

Rushing down the hallway he thought about the money he had stashed in his safety deposit box at the bank. It was Saturday and he couldn't get it that night so the plan was to care for it Monday.

But first he had to get out of town.

The moment he opened the door he saw someone in a black hoodie with white face paint— black around the eyes. Behind the individual were several men, with their hands stuffed in their pockets. He reasoned every one of them had guns and they were all coming for him.

The killer came on behalf of Echo and it appeared Nasir wouldn't be leaving anytime soon.

Slowly the killer raised a weapon and fired six times in his face, taking his life instantly before bending down to whisper "Goon" in his ear.

CHAPTER NINETEEN
BY FORCE

Echo walked into her club after business hours, followed by five bodyguards. Standing in a huddle was Six, Taja and Kari. They were speaking in hushed tones trying to figure out what was happening and why they were meeting at Echo's strip club in the middle of the day.

When Echo approached them she looked back at her men. "Guard the doors. I'll be fine." When they were gone she turned toward her family. "I'm sorry about the last few weeks but it needed to be done."

"That's all you have to say?" Six asked in an angry tone. "You hijack niggas!"

"You look well rested though," Echo said jokingly.

"The shit ain't funny," Six snapped back.

"Yeah, Echo...you kidnapped us and held us up for weeks," Kari said. "We weren't even allowed to see you or talk to our family until tonight."

"I called you everyday to make sure things were cool," Echo said.

"But you never said nothing!" Kari yelled.

"And I think I fucking lost my job," Taja added.

"I'm sorry," she said softly. "I really am. And if there were any other way I would've done it. But I needed to make sure everybody I loved was nowhere to be found. And safe. So I did what I had to do."

"Why Mariah got to stay home then?" Taja asked, crossing her arms over her chest. "Why she not here?"

"Because she needed to stay with Nasir and save face. If I took her too they would've known something was going on."

"So basically she knew why we had to split?" Six asked. "While the rest of us were left in the dark?"

"She wasn't the only one I couldn't find...I couldn't get up with Faith either so I had to worry every day that she was safe while I put the plan into motion."

"So what was the plan?" Six asked.

"Murder." She looked at all of them. "I found out that Sapphire wasn't who she claimed to be."

"We tried to tell you." Six said. "And you act like we didn't put in work together before. I could've helped you."

"I know you, you wouldn't have stayed put, Six. You would've been up under some bitch and got caught slipping. Couldn't take the chance."

Echo continued to give them the entire story and how she learned that Sapphire was Nasir's cousin. It wasn't from Taja, but from Goon. "With the ties Nasir has to the drug game with his father I needed to be sure everybody else I loved was safe." She looked at her sister. "Because I'm almost sure they had something to do with killing ma."

Taja's eyes watered before tears flowed. "So what did you do?"

"Let's just say Nasir won't be a problem anymore."

"How do you know his father won't retaliate like you said?" Kari asked.

"I talked to his pops before doing anything...out of respect for the streets. He knew his son violated and had to pay. At first he offered me some money but there wasn't a big enough number to satisfy. My mother is gone. In the end he paid with his wife and son."

"Man, you could've told us," Taja continued, wiping the tears from her face. "Being taken forcefully and held at gunpoint is scary, Echo."

"I bet it was pretty hard on you with the five star hotels I put you in and all...and the unlimited food and spa treatments." Echo looked at Six. "Oh, let me not forget about the two females I paid to provide you with every pleasure imaginable." She paused. "Let's keep it one hundred, I did right by ya'll and your bank accounts are steady." She looked at each of them in their eyes. "And I would do it again if it meant keeping you safe."

They realized she was right.

"So what now?" Kari asked.

"We go on with our lives," Echo said. When her phone rang she removed it from her purse and put a finger up. "One sec, its Mariah." She stepped a few feet away. "What's up?"

"Echo, you have to come now," she said crying uncontrollably.

Echo's heart thumped. "Where are you?"

"At my parent's house."

"I'm in route! Don't go nowhere!" she threw her cell phone in her purse. "I gotta bounce," Echo told them.

"Before you leave I have to tell you something...about Aspen," Taja said grabbing her arm.

"If it's about Sapphire don't worry, she'll be taken care of tonight." Echo yelled running out the door.

Echo stood in Janice and Rick's bedroom, gazing down at their bodies. Janice had a black tie wrapped tightly around her throat— her face blue as death. Rick suffered a gunshot wound to the chin and Mariah was an emotional wreck. "I don't understand," Echo said softly. "I...I..."

"I told you already!" Mariah yelled. "My mother killed herself and I killed him."

"But why now?"

Mariah walked a few feet away and sat on a black chair next to the door. Echo followed. "He was infected," Mariah said softly.

"With what?"

"HIV..."

Echo's jaw dropped. "For...for how long?"

"Since I was in high school."

Echo leaned against the wall, her blue Hermes bag dropped to the floor. "During the time he was raping you this nigga had the bug?"

She nodded yes. "I'm pretty sure."

"So are you...are you..."

"Infected too?" Mariah shrugged. "I don't know."

Echo looked at the bodies again. Everything in her life was happening too quickly. "What went down tonight?"

"My mother had been sick...couldn't hold down much food. My father said the flu was going around and not to worry, so she didn't. She was always a fool when it came to him. Believing everything he said." she shook her head. "Anyway it's not unusual for my mother to be sick or my father...but this time was different." She paused. "Some weeks back she saw a purple mark on her belly. A few days later another popped up and she went to see a doctor." Tears flooded her eyes. "They were lesions and today she got the results. She's HIV positive."

Echo touched her throbbing forehead and her hand dropped to the side.

"When she brought it up to my father he broke down. Cried about how sorry he was. Said he didn't want her to leave him but he knew all along he had that shit." She looked at his corpse with hate filled eyes. "So I killed him."

"That's why you been asking for fake ID's?"

"I knew I was gonna kill him the moment she was sick and I had to leave town. I knew before my mother did that she was HIV positive. I saw the guilt on his face when he looked at her. I remembered how he fussed over her, doing all he could to make her comfortable."

"I thought you were trying to leave Nasir. That's why you wanted the ID's."

"He wasn't even a factor." She looked into Echo's eyes. "But I am leaving, Echo. Going far away. And before I left I wanted you to know that I always loved you."

"Don't say that—"

"Let me talk...I allowed what he felt about being gay and what he wanted from me sexually to dictate who I loved. As long as he was alive...and judging me, I never felt free enough to be with you. To love who I loved. And now it may be too late."

Echo's eyes widened. "Why?"

"Because if I have HIV, I could never risk giving it to you. It means we can't be together. Ever."

"Maybe that ain't a decision you get to make alone."

"I don't get it?"

Echo sighed. "I care about you. It was never based on if you were sick or well. You the love of my life and always will be." Mariah stood up and they embraced. When her cell rang she sighed, separated from Mariah and reached in her purse on the floor to retrieve the phone. "I'm getting tired of this thing." She answered it. "Hello."

"Echo, come quick!" Faith yelled. "Something happened to Kari...I think Sapphire did it!"

Echo dipped out of the elevator and rushed toward Kari and Faith's apartment. She was so worried that Sapphire got to her friends that she forgot to tell her bodyguards to meet her there.

She banged heavily on the door. "Faith!" she yelled. "Open the door!" she knocked again. "Kari! Anybody home?"

Knock! Knock!

When she realized no one was coming she gambled and twisted the knob, gaining access. Running through the apartment she realized no one was home. Back in the living room she removed her phone from her purse and called Kari, something she should've done before leaving.

The moment Kari answered she was shocked to hear her voice. "Hey, Echo. What's up?"

Frowning she asked, "Where are you?"

"Still at the club with Taja and Six having a few drinks. Why...what's up?"

"You talked to your sister?"

"We got into an argument on the phone...earlier after you left...about her treating my crib like a hotel but that was about it. Ended up telling her to find somewhere else to live." She paused. "Why, what she tell you about it?"

"She called me on some crazy shit."

"Well if you see her can you get my car? When you took us off the streets she had the keys to my Acura the entire time. Who knows what it looks like?"

"I'll see what I can do...let me hit you later." Echo dialed Faith's cell once and no one answered. Worried that Sapphire got to her friend she called her again and this time she answered. "Faith, where are you?"

"I need help...I'm in the parking gar—"

The call ended abruptly and Echo looked at her cell, only to realize the battery was dead. "Fuck!"

She replayed what Faith said in her mind. *"I need help...I'm in the parking gar..."*

"She's in the garage," she said out loud. Before leaving she grabbed her purse, looked inside and made sure bullets were in the chamber of her gun. When she was ready she walked out of the apartment to help her friend.

Sitting in the passenger seat of Kari's Acura, Echo did all she could to calm Faith down to make out what she was saying. "Slower...I can't understand."

Faith took several deep breaths and wiped the tears from her face. "I know, Echo. I know everything."

Frowning she asked, "What are you talking about?"

"I know about Aspen."

"What about her?"

"You killed her didn't you, Echo? You killed her that day and blamed me for it."

For Echo it felt as if the car was spinning and she was beyond confused. "Faith, on everything I love I have no idea what you talking about. I mean I know you said you didn't do it and I looked out for you because I believed you. But you got it fucked up if you think it was me."

"I did fifteen years," she said hysterically. "Five years in juvie before being transferred on account of some shit you did."

"Ain't you listening...I just told you it wasn't me! Who told you this bullshit anyway?"

Faith reached down and grabbed a gun tucked under the seat. Aiming it at Echo she said, "I know you did it. Nobody hated Aspen more than me 'cept you."

Echo was heartbroken. "After everything I did for you, this is how you repay me? You would pull a gun on me, bitch?"

She cocked the weapon.

"Listen, Faith." She raised both hands. "I love you. You're my sister and the last thing I would want is."

"You a fucking liar!" she screamed as her body jerked around.

"I'm not lying! If I murdered her I would've never let you go to jail for my crime! I'm a real bitch about mine and I don't fuck my friends over!"

"Well I don't believe—"

Quicker on the draw, Echo removed her gun from her purse and fired, hitting her in the head. The moment she pulled the trigger she was consumed with remorse. The gun dropped out of her hand and she took several deep breaths. She had no idea what Faith was talking about but she knew she would never be able to live with herself for what she just did.

Just when she thought it couldn't get any worse, Karen, who was sitting in the parked car behind hers, walked along the side of the car and gazed inside.

Echo grabbed her gun and hopped out. "Get in the backseat, bitch!"

"Please, don't shoot," she said with raised arms. "I was just coming to see if anybody needed—"

"Get the fuck in the car!" Echo screamed. "I won't ask you again."

Karen quickly opened the door and eased inside the Acura. Once she was inside, Echo sat in the backseat with the gun still trained in her direction. Karen glanced at the driver's seat and noticed that the woman sitting there was dead. Her head was drooped to the right and blood flowed down her shoulder and onto the carpet.

"Who are you?" Echo asked. "Why are you over here?"

Trembling she said, "I was just...I was just..."

"Getting in business that has nothing to do with you." Her gaze bounced around, as if she would shoot at any minute.

Karen nodded. "I'm so sorry. If you let me leave I won't say anything."

Echo's stance was stiff. "I can't trust you."

"I promise!" Karen pleaded, doing her best to sound confident. "I'll get in my car and go home. And you'll never hear from me again just please don't kill me."

"I don't know you. Even if I wanted to believe you I can't take the risk." she glanced at the corpse. "I knew her for years and I thought I could trust her too." She glanced back at Karen and cocked the weapon. "Look at how she ended up."

Karen began to cry hysterically until the butt of the weapon came crashing down on her forehead, quieting her instantly. "No fucking crying," she yelled.

Karen covered her mouth with both hands.

"I need silence," Echo continued with wild eyes gazing around the car. "I need peace until I can figure all this shit out." She looked deeply into her eyes. "And if you knew me, you'd do well to heed my warning."

"Please...I have a little girl," she continued to plead. If she were going to die it wouldn't be without a fight. "All I do is go to work, come home and take care of her. I'm even in school. Don't take me away from my child when she needs her mother."

Trying to get her mind off the situation for a second she decided to humor her. "Where?"

"Where what?"

"Do you work?"

"It's a new spot called Echo's strip club. I'm a dancer."

Hearing her own name Echo looked at Karen and laughed hysterically. Slowly she lowered the weapon. Although few of the dancers seen her, or knew what she looked like, she had every piece of information on them. She knew the long forms she made them fill out would come in handy but she never predicted it would save a life.

"What's wrong?" Karen asked.

"When you were hired at Echo's you were asked to give five names and addresses of your nearest relatives and five names for your friends." She paused. "That information was verified before we hired you."

Karen's eyes widened. "How did you know?"

"Don't worry...just know that I have more Intel on you than you ever would on me. And if this ever comes out I will find you and kill everyone you know and love. Am I clear?"

"Yes...of course." She nodded hysterically. "This shit here ain't got nothing to do with me and I should've minded my business."

"You'll see me again real soon, just to make sure you remember our agreement." She paused. "Now get out of this fucking car before I change my mind."

When she pulled off, Echo left Faith's body as it was and wiped her fingerprints off everything. Once in her own car, which was parked in the front of the building, she quickly charged her cell. The moment she had one bar she made a call. "Stop that bitch cold, Arnold," she said referring to Sapphire.

"No problem...but someone else wants to get involved," He said. "Your sister."

Frowning she asked, "How she know to contact you?"

"Said when whenever we're together you talk to me the most." He paused. "What you want me to do?"

THE NEXT DAY

Sapphire sat on a cool bench at a park at 5:00 in the morning. She'd been there all night, wondering how she wasted her life. She knew at any moment her time on earth would be over and tried to find a way out of it all. But she was coming up with blanks.

Now lying to Faith about Echo killing Aspen didn't make much sense.

As she saw the sunrise over the horizon, three shiny black unmarked vans pulled up to the park.

Her heart rate increased.

It was time.

Slowly fifteen masked men approached her with Echo in the lead. When they made it to her the goons surrounded the bench and Echo sat next to Sapphire. Looking ahead, Echo leaned back, crossed her legs and sighed. "Why the name Sapphire? Out of all the names?"

"Because they come in different shapes and colors...like me."

Echo looked at her and laughed. "You may have lost some weight but I assure you, that you're still black, bitch." She paused. "Remember when we were kids and you use to talk about your boyfriend Ohcey to Taja? And how much he loved you?"

Sapphire smiled. "Yeah." She nodded. "Drop the 'Y' and Ohcey spells Echo backwards. I was talking about you."

Echo laughed to herself. "Why didn't you tell me? Why you carry shit like you hated me so much?"

"Was afraid to come out I guess." She shrugged. "Everybody's not as brave as you."

"I'm far from brave. Just refuse to live a lie."

"So why are you here, Echo? You gonna kill me in broad daylight? When you know how much I love you?"

"Nope, and none of my men are either." She looked down at her and smiled.

"So what's gonna happen?" Sapphire asked hopeful she would survive after all.

"Well, let me let somebody holla at you right quick." She walked toward the men and one of them pulled off a ski mask. It was Taja.

"So you just wanted to see them kill me?" Sapphire shot off. "Is that it?"

"See you get killed?" Taja laughed. "I'm here to put the work in myself." She turned around to one of Echo's men and received a weapon. Without question she fired once in Sapphire's chest before hitting her head.

CHAPTER TWENTY
TWO MONTHS LATER
INFECTED LOVE

Echo sat with Mariah at a Free HIV clinic in Atlanta Georgia. Mariah wanted to be sure she was as far away from her hometown as possible in case she tested positive.

With her father's death being deemed a murder suicide by the coroner, Mariah was free to live her life but first she needed to know her status.

Sitting in the waiting room with Echo, Mariah looked over at her. She couldn't get over how stunning, strong and powerful Echo had gotten over the years. She was a far cry from the girl she grew up with. "I can't believe you stuck by me...after all of this."

"Why you keep saying that shit?" Echo said seriously. "If you love someone you don't leave if they're sick."

"Even if I'm positive, and you do decide to leave, I wouldn't blame you." She paused. "It's not your fault I'm in this situation."

"It's not yours either...you were raped."

"I'm serious, Echo!"

"And so am I!" She looked ahead and then at her again. "My entire life I loved one woman. Some people have more experiences, but for me it's always been you."

"But you were about to marry Sapphire," she joked.

"I wasn't gonna marry that bitch," she laughed. "Figured you would crash the wedding anyway." She laughed. "Look, I made some mistakes but I'm not making anymore. And I'm not gonna let the love of my life ride this shit alone if I can help it. I'm a rich woman and if you do have HIV I want everyday to be a celebration. Besides, it's not the death sentence it used to be."

A tear rolled from Mariah's eye. "I can't believe I almost let you get away."

"But you didn't."

Mariah looked out into the busy clinic. Everybody appeared worried. Just when her mind wandered to how terrible her life would be if she tested positive, Echo grabbed her hand placing her at ease.

Twenty minutes later the nurse called Mariah's name. "Here goes...," she said. "Wish me luck."

"You'll be fine," Echo said.

As she disappeared in the back Echo thought about all the fun they had over the past few months.

Although Faith's murder was ruled drug related due to her habit, Echo, Maria, Kari, Six and Taja somehow managed to grow closer. An unspoken bond between them developed and they knew no matter what they would have each other's backs. And even if Mariah had HIV, Echo would never leave her side.

When time continued to tick by and she hadn't returned Echo resigned to the fact that she was positive. It was now time to create an action plan to get her the best care.

Fifteen minutes later Mariah came outside with a smile on her face. Walking up to her she said, "Negative!"

Echo exhaled and tried to appear calm, as if she'd always known the results would be in her favor. "Well...what took you so long?"

"The nurse is pregnant...stopped by the bathroom to throw up for fifteen minutes before telling me anything. Drove me crazy waiting!" she laughed.

Echo stood up. "What now?"

Mariah walked closer and kissed her on the lips. "Well, let's start by going to your place and me giving you a long bath."

Mariah looped her arm around hers like she did when they were kids as they walked toward the exit. "Oh yeah? Then what?"

"Well," Mariah winked. "Then I'm gonna lay you on the bed, lotion your sexy body, spread your legs apart and lick you clean."

Echo blushed. "Word? You gonna do all that?"

"I'm not done. And then I'm gonna fall asleep eating your pussy."

They reached the Porsche limo. "And why do I deserve all that?"

"Because I never got a chance to show you how I feel about you." She winked sliding inside. Echo eased in behind her. "But now you gonna see."

"Garcon, hit it to my place quick!" Echo yelled. "We got some business to 'tend to!"

THE END

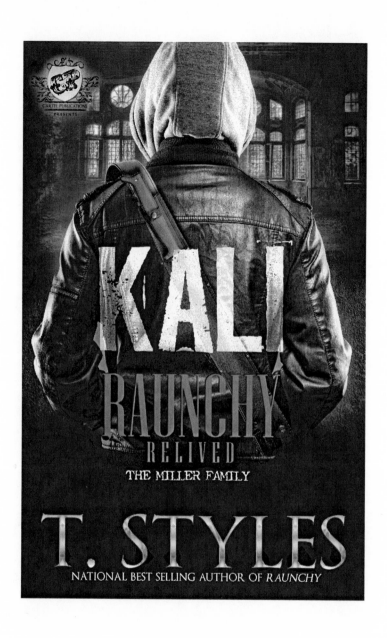

The Cartel Publications Order Form
www.thecartelpublications.com
Inmates **ONLY** receive novels for $10.00 per book.
(Mail Order **MUST** come from inmate directly to receive discount)

Shyt List 1 _____	$15.00
Shyt List 2 _____	$15.00
Shyt List 3 _____	$15.00
Shyt List 4 _____	$15.00
Shyt List 5 _____	$15.00
Pitbulls In A Skirt _____	$15.00
Pitbulls In A Skirt 2 _____	$15.00
Pitbulls In A Skirt 3 _____	$15.00
Pitbulls In A Skirt 4 _____	$15.00
Victoria's Secret _____	$15.00
Poison 1 _____	$15.00
Poison 2 _____	$15.00
Hell Razor Honeys _____	$15.00
Hell Razor Honeys 2 _____	$15.00
A Hustler's Son 2 _____	$15.00
Black and Ugly As Ever _____	$15.00
Year Of The Crackmom _____	$15.00
Deadheads _____	$15.00
The Face That Launched A _____	$15.00
Thousand Bullets	
The Unusual Suspects _____	$15.00
Miss Wayne & The Queens of DC _____	$15.00
Paid In Blood (eBook Only) _____	$15.00
Raunchy _____	$15.00
Raunchy 2 _____	$15.00
Raunchy 3 _____	$15.00
Mad Maxxx _____	$15.00
Quita's Dayscare Center _____	$15.00
Quita's Dayscare Center 2 _____	$15.00
Pretty Kings _____	$15.00
Pretty Kings 2 _____	$15.00
Pretty Kings 3 _____	$15.00
Silence Of The Nine _____	$15.00
Silence Of The Nine 2 _____	$15.00
Prison Throne _____	$15.00
Drunk & Hot Girls _____	$15.00
Hersband Material _____	$15.00
The End: How To Write A _____	$15.00
Bestselling Novel In 30 Days (Non-Fiction Guide)	
Upscale Kittens _____	$15.00

Lipstick Dom

Wake & Bake Boys	_____	$15.00
Young & Dumb	_____	$15.00
Young & Dumb 2:	_____	$15.00
Tranny 911	_____	$15.00
Tranny 911: Dixie's Rise	_____	$15.00
First Comes Love, Then Comes Murder	_____	$15.00
Luxury Tax	_____	$15.00
The Lying King	_____	$15.00
Crazy Kind Of Love	_____	$15.00
And They Call Me God	_____	$15.00
The Ungrateful Bastards	_____	$15.00
Lipstick Dom	_____	$15.00

Please add $4.00 **PER BOOK** for shipping and handling.

The Cartel Publications * P.O. BOX 486 OWINGS MILLS MD 21117

Name: _____

Address: _____

City/State: _____

Contact# & Email:

_____

Please allow 5-7 BUSINESS days before shipping. The Cartel is NOT responsible for prison orders rejected.

<u>*NO PERSONAL CHECKS ACCEPTED*</u>

By T. Styles   213

CPSIA information can be obtained at www.ICGtesting.com
Printed in the USA
LVOW11s1708131115

462469LV00001B/197/P